THE VULCAN BULLETINS

SAM GULLIVER

SIMON AND SCHUSTER · NEW YORK

SBN 671–21665–1
LIBRARY OF CONGRESS CATALOG CARD NUMBER: 73–13580
DESIGNED BY EVE METZ
MANUFACTURED IN THE UNITED STATES OF AMERICA

1   2   3   4   5   6   7   8   9   10

FOR JAMES HALE,
WITH AFFECTION AND THANKS

1

My flight to Hamburg didn't leave until four o'clock that afternoon, so even after a slow stroll across Blackheath I decided I would still have ample time to call in at the shop en route for the air terminal. I like the heath because it's ten degrees colder there than anywhere else in London and I find invigorating the unexpected bald expanse in the middle of dense urban sprawl. By the time I'd reached Holborn and was walking up Portugal Street with my overnight bag in one hand, I was in one of those springy, optimistic moods that so seldom outlive the lunchtime drink.

The shop's modest, I will admit, and there's no discreetly handsome gold lettering above its single narrow display window. In fact, the name was blocked out in white paint with a stencil. LEE & SAVERNAKE, it said. Lee referred to me; Savernake was a figment, the only pretentious thing about the place. A friend had advised me to invent a partner because people liked their friendly local firearms dealer to have a hint of the old-established about him. It may even be true.

There was nobody inside the shop but Moleman, ex-safecracker and personal assistant. He was dusting off the hand-guns beneath the glass-topped counter.

"Morning, Mole," I said. "How's business?"

"Nobody been in but the postman," he told me.

"Things'll pick up come the silly season."

"It's arrived already," said Moleman, "but I'd forgotten. We did have one customer a couple of hours ago."

"Could we help him?"

"No. I couldn't find your stock of one-seven-seven ammunition."

"We don't have any, that's why."

"So I told him. He was eleven. He also wanted to know how to make his air rifle more powerful."

"Local vicar getting a bit out of hand?"

"No, pigeons," said Moleman. "He told me he could hit 'em all right, but they wouldn't drop dead."

"Not enough mass in one-seven-sevens. Tough feathers, pigeons have. I expect the slugs were bouncing off."

"Well," said Moleman, "he said if you got them up the arse the slugs go in, but the bloody bird would just fly off. So far he'd only come up with one answer."

"Which was?" I asked, going through the post with one hand.

"He raided the bathroom cupboard, found his mother's sleeping tablets, ground 'em up and filled the slugs with the powder. As I stand here, Lee, that kid was shooting pellets stuffed with Mandrax up pigeons' bottoms."

"Ingenious. Did it work?"

"Jesus, Lee, how do I know? He *said* it did, but kids are such damn liars anyway. He claimed the things were falling asleep in midair all over Bromley."

8

"I think you've just missed recruiting a future member of the Javits Corporation, Mole," I told him. "Inventive and enterprising."

"I wouldn't let my kid do things like that and that's a fact."

There was the usual crop of magazines and catalogues, mostly from the States. *Gun World Summary, Law Enforcement Digest, Handgun Monthly*. I tossed them to one side for when I had time to catch up on essential reading and opened a letter postmarked Tripoli.

"You remember Selby?" I asked Moleman when I'd read it.

"Your mate in the Middle East?"

"That's the one. He's coming to London in the next day or two. Says he wants to see me so he'll be dropping by the shop. If I'm not back, tell him I'm on a quick job and to stick around for forty-eight hours. That's at the outside," I added. "I should be back the day after tomorrow."

"Okay, Lee, I'll hold the fort. If anything urgent crops up, where'll you be?"

"Try the Corporation's branch in Hamburg," I said. "I'm giving a lecture-demonstration on the Thompson in Heligoland tomorrow, at Javits' personal request. To the Provisional IRA."

"Holy Mary" was all Moleman said.

Like a lot of ex-cons, Moleman was curiously conservative in some ways. I reflected on this in the airport bus, thinking that it maybe contributed to the sense of security I felt whenever I had to leave him in charge of the shop. He could be relied on to do nothing rash. True, he was more ignorant about firearms than I'd have liked, but then I'm a fanatic. Mole's talent—apart from the safe-breaking, which he had

9

renounced on becoming a family man—was as a middle-man for some of my private deals. He was solid and astute, and even some of the guys in the arms trade trusted him.

The flight to Hamburg was uneventful, which is to say that I arrived in one piece. I rang up Herold in the office and found I was booked in at the Altona. Herold was a fattish man who ran the German branch of the Javits Corporation.

"Nothing but the best, Herr McGundrell." He had a voice like a butter slide.

"Extravagant," I told him, "quite apart from being uncomfortable. Icy chambermaids and overheated rooms. I'll find my own place."

"Hm." Herold clearly thought I was lowering the Company tone. "As you wish. You will be coming in tomorrow?"

"I can hardly do the demonstration without a weapon, Herold."

"I shall have one waiting. Also ammunition and a van."

I'd been working for the Javits Corporation for three years, but I'd met Javits himself before that, when I was in the Army. I was posted to Malaysia to assist with the small-arms training at Tekong Balau, and there was this unforgettable albino black with crinkly ginger hair and white eyelashes like a pig's. He turned out to be an American named Javits who'd mysteriously flown in with a Special Forces unit from Vietnam. He didn't seem to be military—which, knowing the U.S. forces and their hangers-on, probably made him an Agency man or Free Enterprise. After seeing him around for a few days I plumped for the second, although with the American Government, service and free-booting are not mutually exclusive.

At any rate, Javits seemed to like my small-arms training

sessions, for not long after leaving the Army I went to work for him. As far as I could gather, he himself had started in a small way, touring Europe in late 1945 buying up weapons, renovating many of them himself and stockpiling them until he had an extensive private collection of highly salable guns. By the time I met him, the Javits Corporation, although its registered Head Office was in Illinois, had several branches in Europe, and Javits himself had taken up permanent residence in Vienna. Judged by the standards of Sam Cummings and Interarms, the company was still not large, but Javits' contacts were excellent, and he had a good few thousand square feet of warehousing facilities in several countries. His intelligence system also seemed to be outstanding; either that or he had an uncanny amount of luck. His deals almost never fell through, and I'd noticed that his knowledge of whom to approach and when seemed almost inspired sometimes.

It had taken me a little over eighteen months to become Javits' man in the U.K. I found myself in charge of a small office near Haymarket and a warehouse in Shadwell. But because you can never predict the vagaries of fate and cardiac trouble, I began saving hard to form my own small business by way of added security. I'll admit now that when Javits accused me of creaming off some of the profits that might properly have gone to the Corporation I pleaded guilty. But as I pointed out at the time, it was always money I'd earned over and above the sales figures we'd agreed on: perhaps by taking a bit of commission in exchange for a personal favor I'd done the client; perhaps simply by using facilities as basic as the Corporation's headed notepaper. I hardly ever stole so much as a ten-pound note.

All in all, I think Javits approved, because he appreciated

private enterprise. He made it clear that as long as my activities didn't interfere with what he was paying me for, then my own affairs weren't any of his business. He was wrong; but because I wasn't born yesterday there was nothing to show for it. Nothing, that is, except Lee & Savernake.

2

The next day it was just like the Army all over again, except that I was talking to eight members of the Provisional IRA. But the scenery couldn't have been improved on. Two o'clock on a cold November afternoon on the west coast of Schleswig-Holstein about forty miles south of the Danish border, scudding gray clouds overhead and a biting wind coming off the North Sea and Heligoland Bay. It whistled through the stiff tussocks of marram grass dotted along the desolate foreshore before rattling the panes in the windows of the long, low indoor range.

The Provos were buying automatic weapons from Javits—a ridiculously small order by most standards, but just the sort of thing he was not too grand to deal with. What he was also supplying was a sort of presales service, in this case my demonstration on the history, working and care of the Thompson submachine gun. McNeill, one of the Irishmen, had explained over lunch that although plenty of his men knew how to squeeze a trigger, few of them knew much about the principle or maintenance of the weapons they used. This led to a great deal of inefficiency. The Army had noticed the bad condition of many of the weapons they captured. Quite a few had jammed in action and been abandoned because the operator had to make a getaway and had been unable to clear the gun in a hurry. The increase in armed IRA activity over the previous couple of years had led to a score of offers from all sorts of people in the arms trade, but many of the IRA who knew about weapons had been killed or captured, and gradually the whole issue had hinged around supply routes rather than the choice of weapons. Now a policy decision had meant more careful buying of weapons, greater standardization and better training.

"Right, gentlemen," I said. "I've been asked by Major McNeill to assume you know nothing about the Thompson or its principle and to start from scratch. No problem, because it's a nice easy weapon, but I realize some of you will already be familiar with it. If there's anything you'd like to add to what I say, any suggestions arising from having used the gun in combat situations, please don't hesitate.

"The design of the Thompson is quite old and it's still being made in its last modification, so that means it's a good, reliable weapon. As far as I remember, the prototype appeared way back in 1919, but the first production model came out in 1921. There were several models during the Twenties, some of different caliber. The most common Thompson models are those chambered for the forty-five ACP cartridge. ACP stands for Automatic Colt Pistol, as you no doubt know, and the forty-five ACP is the cartridge that fits the Government Model Colt forty-five—the standard side arm of the U.S. forces.

"The first two important Thompson models were those of 1921 and 1928. These were the ones that achieved a certain notoriety by being associated with Chicago gangsters, and the typical Tommy gun of the period has a pistol grip for the left hand ahead of the magazine as well as a barrel with cooling fins on it. Most of them were also fitted with an optional Cutts compensator on the muzzle. Are you gentlemen familiar with the principle of the Cutts compensator?" I looked round at their faces as they sat on folding chairs grouped round the firing point of the range.

"It's to stop muzzle climb," said McNeill.

"Right," I said. "On full auto fire the muzzle of a weapon tends to climb, so your shots get higher and higher. This is difficult to control and wasteful, so the compensator was invented to overcome it. It consists of a number of parallel, backward-slanting cuts made into the top part of the muzzle. The cuts go down to the bore, and the principle is that when the back end of the bullet is just leaving the muzzle, some of the gas pressure in the barrel behind it escapes through these vents, blowing the muzzle downwards and slightly forwards. The principle works: you'll often see compensators used in match pistols. The only trouble is that you lose some velocity.

"Now, the other thing you'll see in pictures of Tommy guns as used by U.S. bootleggers is the circular drum-type magazine. These were of two kinds, fifty-shot and one-hundred-shot. The hundred-shot magazine was not really practicable, because the feeding was never a hundred percent reliable, and anyway, a hundred forty-five ACP rounds weigh upwards of four and a half pounds, which is a hell of a weight to hang under a submachine gun.

"Then in 1942 the Americans modified the Thompson again and adopted if for military use in a big way. The British Government had by then placed large orders for the 1928 model, although a lot of the guns they bought are now at the bottom of the Atlantic because they were being shipped over at the time when the German U-boat campaign was at its height. Anyway, this new Thompson model was called the M-1. The main differences were that it had the charging handle—or actuator knob, or cocking handle, depending on what you want to call it—taken off the top of the gun and put on to the right side; it also had a simpler rear sight. Shortly afterwards came the last real design change—the M1A1, which is exactly the same as the M-1 except that now the firing pin doesn't move: it's a little bump machined onto the bolt face.

"This is the gun you've just bought, the M1A1," I said, picking up the demonstration weapon from the table beside me. "It's an already sound design simplified as much as it can be. Straight blowback principle. Dead easy. Questions?"

I looked round. The wind was buffeting the windows in their rusty metal frames, and I caught occasional glimpses of sea gulls being blown diagonally across the gray sky outside. Somebody leaned down and turned up the wick of a paraffin heater on the floor. It didn't do much to drive the cold out of this roofed concrete alley with its pile of damp sand twenty-five yards down the far end behind the target holders.

"Okay. We'd better be sure of stripping the gun, then, but first I'd like to say a few elementary things about gun care, because it's obvious from weapons I've seen used by allegedly competent units that a lot of people don't know the first thing about it." I was beginning to get back in my old Army lecture-room swing now, and rather enjoying it.

"Firstly, no gun will shoot accurately if you allow lead fouling to build up in the barrel. Ordinary deposits won't make much difference, but lead will. But more importantly, there's the question of rust. Most people believe that the danger of rust magically disappeared with the introduction of noncorrosive primers and smokeless powder. This is cock. You lot in particular will have to watch out, though, because you might find yourselves using pre-1952 ACP rounds. After that date most factories making ordnance changed over to noncorrosive primers. But before that, the primers contained potassium chlorate, which gave up its oxygen on detonation and left potassium chloride behind. Potassium chloride is very like sodium chloride, or common table salt, in that it attracts water, which in turns leads to rust. So watch your ammunition. If it's earlier than 1952, pay special attention to cleaning."

"What have noncorrosive primers got in them?" someone asked. I grimaced.

"I'm pretty bad at chemistry," I said. "They aren't all the same, of course. Different factories use different compounds. But most of them include stuff called lead styphnate and also ground glass. The glass alone is a good reason for cleaning weapons, because it gets deposited on friction surfaces and causes wear."

"What in hell do they put ground glass in for?"

"Apparently it's essential because only it will cause the friction that provides enough concentrated heat to ensure successful detonation every time. It's the reliability factor. Anyway, these are all good reasons for cleaning your weapon—especially a fully automatic gun with parts that have large arcs of movement.

"Now, field-stripping the M1A1." I picked up the weapon again. "First, remove the magazine by pressing the catch up with your thumb and just pulling the magazine down and out. Like this." I held the weapon up so everybody could see and removed the box magazine. "Secondly, check that the bolt is *forward*. You strip the 1928 model with the bolt back and the weapon cocked, but not this one—okay? Now, turn the gun upside down on a flat surface and with a screwdriver or something push in the receiver locking catch at the back here. Then, while pressing the trigger you can pull the whole gun neatly into two parts, like this. See? The butt-and-trigger assembly slides away from the barrel and the receiver. You'll find there are some guides in the receiver here and here which slot into these lips on the frame.

"Next you tackle the bit containing the buffer pilot and recoil spring . . ." I was safely away, doing what I enjoyed. Perhaps some of them found it boring, but it didn't show, so they were either strangely polite or convinced that the knowledge might all contribute to keeping them alive. One or two may even have found it beautiful, the way the weapon falls neatly apart into eight pieces. They're very well made, those Thompsons. Even the early models, way back in the 1920s, sold for two hundred dollars.

After that, we went out to do some practice firing. It was beginning to get dark by now, but they all of them tried to put some rounds into a tussock at various ranges. It was notable that even a couple of the Provisionals who'd been in combat situations with the British Army mishandled their weapons. It's a common fallacy that with a fully automatic gun like the Thompson all you have to do is go into a gunslinger's crouch, hold the thing at waist level and hose the target down, being certain of at least a few hits. The IRA must have been shooting off a hell of a lot of ammunition without much result. The Thompson has a good barrel length and is potentially an accurate weapon at a hundred yards or more. If fired properly from the shoulder, it'll hit what you want it to. And the trick to counteracting muzzle climb is to fire in short bursts of three to five shots before reaiming.

When it was too dark to see, we locked up the indoor range, climbed into the Volkswagen minibus and bumped off down the track to the nearest village, Wilhelmsbüttel. There the Provisionals insisted on stopping for quantities of beer— to keep the cold out, as they put it—before heading back to Javits' base in Hamburg. We chatted a bit while I drank Glühwein and ate pieces of smoked eel. I felt rather sober as I drove the eight singing Irishmen back down the Elbe estuary to Hamburg.

"All okay?" asked Herold when I got into the office. The German branch of the Javits Corporation was this lushly appointed office in the city center together with a warehouse in the port. Herold took the Thompson from me, together with a box of unused ammunition.

"Fine. They've all gone off to see a blue movie or something. They like what they've bought. Eighty submachine guns is hardly the largest deal the Corporation's ever handled, but it's sure got some enthusiastic buyers. When do the guns go?"

"Tomorrow."

"Reykjavik to Shannon?"

"Yes. Here to Iceland as BMW shock absorbers and from Iceland to Eire as volcanic-rock samples for the geology department of Trinity College, Dublin."

I nodded. Herold locked the Thompson away in a steel cabinet.

"Meanwhile," he said, "you must try what Hamburg has to offer before you go home, Mr. McGundrell. It's a wonderful place; we've everything here."

"It's hardly my first visit, Herold, as you bloody well know." Extraordinary how people always try to sell you their hometowns, and especially in that salacious way. I imagined trying to convince a tourist that my own birthplace, Canterbury, was a depraved, wide-open city. The only time I've found the boast justified was in Bangkok, where, thanks to the stimulus of the need to cater to American GIs far enough from home to be safely out of Mama's sight, an industry was in full swing to satisfy any imaginable appetite for any conceivable experience. It was just a question of cash, but with cash whatever you wanted was available.

I wandered around Hamburg feeling immensely cold. It was certainly true that since leaving the Army it was the evenings I enjoyed least. I seemed always to be eating alone in restaurants, having first remembered to buy a newspaper or a book to read. Tonight I found myself glumly turning the pages of *The Agony and the Ecstasy* and eating something they called a "Schlachtplatte"—which would translate heartily as a "battle trencher," though it was not easy to tell if it was a dish designed to give you strength or whether the battle referred simply to the struggle it took to get through it. A vast plate piled with about six different types of boiled sausage with tight transparent skins which enabled you to see bubbles chasing each other under the surface if you prodded them. Plus more mashed potatoes than could be comfortably lifted. After this, I staggered through the streets and ran into one of the Provisionals I'd helped check out on the Thompson that afternoon. He was alone and disgruntled. He said he'd never been in such a sinful place and that he couldn't wait to get back to Ireland. There was, he said, a feeling of energy self-indulgently wasted all around him, so he stomped off back to his hotel. Killers are often like that, I've found. He was probably extremely fond of animals, too.

A roaring crowd of merchant seamen being sick over the edge of the pavement was enough to remind me that Hamburg in winter is a place where pleasure, such as it is, is confined indoors. It was several months since my last visit, so I thought listlessly that I might as well see what was new in Europe's fastest-growing industry. I found a brightly lit shop called "Super PornoMarkt" and went in among the few customers flicking through passionless erotica. Spying what I was looking for, I put a handful of marks down on the counter and said "Film," pointing towards a curtained door at the back of the room.

The girl behind the counter was dark and pretty and about as exciting as a rocking horse. *"Bitte hineingehen,"* she said from her post among the tubes of lubricant, whips, rubber cocks and jokey condoms with ears on them. I went behind the curtain and found a small room with a dozen canvas-seated chairs and a projector. The projector was whirring away, and this was the only sound in the room, because blue films are made without sound tracks. On the screen an Alsatian dog and a woman were sniffing at each other, and in what light they shed I could see that only half the seats were filled. After about five minutes, the dog and the woman tired of each other and the projectionist changed the reel.

"Schüler-Sex," said the titles, *"Spermaspritzende Jungen."* I wondered why they always started with bicycles and

21

glanced towards the doorway. The curtain was pushed aside briefly and two people came in, but they were just silhouettes against the bright neon of the shop beyond. They came and sat next to me and turned out to be a man and a woman, who watched stolidly and broke the silence by scrabbling in a box of chocolates from time to time. Meanwhile, the boys on the screen went rollicking on amid Black Forest scenery, doing things with fir cones I wouldn't have thought possible, let alone comfortable. When *"Honeymoon-Sex"* came on I'd had blue films up to here and slipped out, blinking in the fluorescent brilliance of the shop. I strode out past the racks of magazines and into the street.

Nothing new, I thought as I walked back to the hotel. One way and another, it'd been a typical day in the life of an arms dealer, complete with tired executives' pleasures. I went early to bed, depressed and full of wind from the dinner, a costive old businessman like any other.

3

On the plane back to London, I wondered vaguely what Selby wanted to see me about. I didn't suppose it would be of much interest; it was all business nowadays. I so seldom did anything with guns other than cross them off inventories that the IRA demonstration had come as a welcome change. I missed handling the weapons I sold. Staring out of the aircraft's window at the carpet of cloud over the North Sea, I remembered the thousands of happy hours I had spent as a child wandering over the Scotland Hills at the back of Canterbury, watching the Buffs training national servicemen on their firing ranges and assault courses. Those November afternoons when I would give school a miss and worm under the rusty barbed-wire fence at the end of our street on to the chalky hills littered with old ammo boxes, lumps of concrete with bent iron reinforcing rods sticking out, spent cartridges and the pins of practice grenades. I was seldom caught and became good at shadowing platoons on their way from the barracks to the ranges and back again. I would lie in bushes and damp clumps of bracken listening to the lectures and demonstrations, making notes of all the different kinds of weapons and transport I had seen. By about four in the evening the light was getting bad, the platoons would march down again and the hills would be deserted until the following morning unless there were night exercises. Then I would scramble out of my hiding place and make for the nearest range, climbing the steep hills of the butts, sifting handfuls of sand for spent rounds.

It was not long before I became familiar with every type of ammunition used. On the short ranges there was a lot of lead from .22 bullets, mixed up with the 9mm jacketed Parabellum rounds used in automatic weapons like Stens and Sterlings. Occasionally there would be pistol rounds as well, mostly .38 or .45. On the long ranges I could find practically nothing but .303s until the old No. 4 Mark I rifle started to be replaced by the L1A1, when the 7.62mm NATO rounds began to appear.

However familiar I became with these limited varieties of bullet, I never lost the feeling of excited satisfaction when I unearthed a complete specimen. This was quite frequent, because even when fired into sand at more than two thousand feet per second, military metal-jacketed rounds often do not break up at all. Indeed, it has largely been up to civilian law-enforcement authorities such as the U.S. police departments to show that if you want people to stay down when they are hit, you need a round that breaks up on hitting flesh as well as bone. That way all the kinetic energy is delivered at once. Energy that makes a neat hole right through and keeps the bullet going for another half mile is completely wasted.

I would return home at sunset, pockets heavy with brass and copper and lead—down from the hills, slipping and sliding on the early dew, the gray tower of the cathedral sticking out of the town below and the rooks so high in the bald Kentish skies they ought to have been leaving vapor trails. Down to tea at five-thirty, when the Old Man got in from work, the lights yellow behind the curtains of Jubilee Terrace, the smell of sausages and tea. Then up to my bedroom to add my newest finds to my extensive private collection of British Army property.

By the time I was twelve I could, from sheer observation, have field-stripped any of the Army's basic small arms better than anybody other than the instructors. The clueless National Service draftees who would probably be sent in a month or two to point their Sterlings at the Mau Mau fumbled at their weapons, having to learn parrot fashion or by mnemonics the right order in which to take apart beautifully constructed machinery. The instructors cursed, and hidden in the bushes, I cursed with them. I longed for the moment when I could get my own hands on a gun. Then one day towards the end of the Fifties, I did.

Right in the center of the city there was a classy school. You could see the boys all over the place in a sort of fancy dress—kids wearing straw boaters and wing collars and pin-striped trousers, marching around town three abreast making little cuts at people's shins with their walking sticks. One of the games laid on for these middle-class delinquents was playing at soldiers. Sometimes, wearing uniforms and carrying old Lee-Enfield No. 1 Mark IIIs, they would be marched up to the barracks of the Buffs—the Royal East Kent Regiment—where for an afternoon they would be subjected to withering contempt. There were lots of good laughs for me and my mates. Whenever we heard the school band, we used to run up to Scotland Hills and listen to those kids being instructed by regulars who'd obviously been told to tone it down a bit. Even so, they could often make some

25

of the boys cry just by shouting at them, and one or two of the younger ones went all sorts of colors whenever buggery was mentioned.

This school had an armory in which it kept a few hundred ancient Lee-Enfields, some Brens and one or two Stens. Apparently one day their captain of shooting had just locked the door after checking his team's rifles when up drew a couple of Royal Electrical and Mechanical Engineers lorries.

"Afternoon," says a sergeant, jumping out. "Would you mind opening up again? We've come to collect some of your stuff for reconditioning at the depot in Deal"—and he waves a sheet of paper. The captain of shooting isn't too sure of his ground. There's nobody around, and the school Regimental Sergeant-Major has given him strict instructions about never letting unauthorized personnel into the armory.

"I don't think I could do that, sir," he says bravely. The sergeant's tone changes.

"What rank are you when you're in uniform, lad?" he asks with a bit of a cutting edge.

"Corporal, sir."

"What do you see here?" The sergeant taps his chevrons with a thick forefinger.

"Three stripes, Sergeant."

"Right, lad. Open up."

"Yes, sir. Of course, sir." The captain of shooting comes to attention in his pin-striped trousers and his wing collar and opens the armory door. In a couple of minutes the sergeant and three lance corporals remove two truckloads of weapons and ammunition.

"The depot will notify your RSM tomorrow, lad," says the sergeant, climbing back into his truck. "We should have the lot done inside a week." He lets in the clutch and the two

REME trucks drive off, leaving the captain of shooting feeling proud at having used his initiative and taken a responsible decision all on his own.

Which was how the IRA made off with a great number of weapons and ammunition—but in their eagerness to get away took a wrong turn which led them up Jubilee Terrace, deadest of dead ends. I was just coming back from school when I saw these two REME lorries doing a rapid turn in front of our house before tearing off. They turned so rapidly, in fact, that a Sten fell over the tailboard of the last and clattered onto the pavement at my feet. I yelled a bit, but neither lorry stopped, so I grabbed the Sten as if it were made of solid gold, shoved it under my coat and took it home to my bedroom. There I stripped it, smelling the oil and handling the parts with an excitement I can remember to this day. I can also remember my dad's face when he came in and saw me sitting on the edge of my bed reassembling the weapon.

We took it round to the Buffs and they looked a bit worried until they checked the serial number and found that it wasn't one of theirs. They called the police, and the story gradually emerged. Despite a lot of telephoning and general alerts, the IRA team were never caught; neither were many of the weapons recovered, except a few that were turned over to the Welsh Nationalists some years later. Although I had done nothing to merit a reward, I was taken up to the Buffs' barracks for a day and shown over the ranges during practice firing. I went "ooh" and "ahh" at the right moments, not thinking it politic to mention that I had seen it all before many times from not much more than thirty yards away at any given spot. However, I got to look at a newish FN rifle and took it apart, which surprised them. I drank Army tea, said "fuck" a few times and used a field telephone. It was a big deal. But it confirmed my desire to join the Army. I believed in it—and in a way, I still do.

One other thing emerged from this episode and that was the name of the luckless, outranked, beautifully spoken captain of shooting who had opened the armory door to the nice IRA sergeant. His name was Timothy Anscudden, and according to the local paper, he badly wanted a commission. He got one.

We landed at Heathrow just after noon, and Lee & Savernake were closed for the lunch Moleman was eating inside. His wife always sent him with sandwiches; these he spread out over the display counter in neat piles, cheese in one and egg mayonnaise in another.

"You've sold the Remington," I said approvingly. "Somebody wanted a sporting rifle."

"Right you are," said Moleman. "Feller walked in yesterday and took it straight out of the window. 'Been looking for one of them,' he said. 'Particularly wanted a . . . a . . .'" Moleman's voice trailed off, and he lifted a sandwich apologetically. "Can't remember the bloody model," he said.

"Seven eighty-eight," I told him. "I didn't think we'd get rid of it so easily. I suppose he noticed it was left-handed?"

Moleman nodded. "That's what he was looking for. Knew a lot about them, he did. Said Remington only introduced the left-handed version in 1969. He was right, too; I looked it up after he'd gone. So he bought it there and then: cash on the nail."

"Amazing. Anything else? Did Selby call?"

"Not yet. An African gent wanted a word with you this morning, though."

"Oh? What did he want?"

"Wouldn't say," said Moleman, shaking his head and chewing. "Name of Chinde. He left a phone number and said it wasn't vital."

"Those are the ones you kick yourself for not ringing," I assured him. "A couple of months later you read all about the revolution in Africa and wonder which lucky bugger landed their arms order. Do you reckon it was one of those, or merely a fat cat who wanted to shoot gazelles from the back of his Land-Rover?"

"I heard something from a friend," said Moleman with studied vagueness, "and he suggested there was a rumor that Frelimo was in town and buying."

"The Mozambique Liberation Front," I mused. "Could be. Though I wonder why they're not in Hamburg; it's a better toy center. Oh well, I'll check it out. Otherwise nix?"

"Not a sausage. Very quiet."

"Okay, Mole. You can lock up and take the rest of the day off if you want," I said. "Meanwhile, I suppose I'd better go up to the office and do the job I'm drawing a salary for."

4

I joined up in 1963, when I was sixteen. The Thanet Fusiliers was arguably not the Army's most distinguished regiment, but I didn't much care about that. Instead of the drunken rows at home and the long periods on Assistance because my old man was inside or had simply run off, there was orderliness and regular pay. You knew who your friends were, you knew you would be fed and clothed and you also knew that within the hierarchical system there was equity of treatment. You were exactly the equal of your mates. No time wasted having crises of identity or worrying about status or going it alone: none of those petit-bourgeois preoccupations. In that respect, the forces at any given level are like miniature socialist states; it is only when they are viewed from top to bottom that the idea of equality takes a knock.

All this meant that I was free to get interested in what I wanted, which was weaponry. I was a know-all from the first, because I really did have the information. After basic training, I began specializing and narrowly escaped becoming an armorer. The frustration of having to do all that benchwork while scarcely firing a shot would have had me up the wall. Instead, I was trained as a small-arms instructor. By the end of 1965 I had a stripe and they sent the Thanets off to Aden. It was my first combat experience, and I liked it, although it's a fact that you have to get your ideas sorted out in order not to spend your time standing in the Medical Officer's queue asking for tranquilizers or having crying jags in bed. When it's purely a question of personal survival, there are no problems; nobody wrestles with their conscience on a battlefield. It is equally simple in other respects. The Army was what the government could rely on to implement its political decisions, and the British Government had been democratically elected. That was enough for me. It was not a matter for ethics.

What *could* become an ethical question was the methods used. I'm against unnecessary violence not because it's nasty but because it is unprofessional and inefficient, and that was why I was against the little public-school prick who went mad on night patrols in the Crater district. It took me a month or two to link Captain Anscudden with the eighteen-year-old who had briefly hit the news in the *Kentish Gazette* a few years back, but once I remembered where I'd heard the name before, I knew I was right. A couple of overheard conversations with fellow officers about the Dear Old School Days confirmed it.

Captain Anscudden looked just how a young career officer ought to look if one took the criteria of British Lion films. Tallish, thinnish, pinkish and blondish, he had the desperately pale eyes of a maniac. It was not known how he thought that once his men had seen him interrogating Arab suspects they would ever again look at him without wondering a bit. He used to carry a short cane on patrol and usually had to wipe off the last eight inches of it before returning to barracks. His forays into the Arab quarter became known as "Anscudden's panty-raids," which showed an intuitive choice of the correct pathological image. But Anscudden was a snob as well as a shit. "One stends to attention when speaking to an awfficer" became adopted as his catchphrase, and he himself was just the sort of man who stood to attention when telephoning a superior.

It was unfortunate that Captain Anscudden should have been present just as I was admonishing the guardroom at large one afternoon. "One stends to attention," I said nasally, "particularly when speaking to an awfficer of the IRA." The suddenness with which the guffaws had died made me turn round. In the doorway stood Anscudden, pale eyes stony and with little white patches round his nostrils.

It's a long story how things escalated between us, but the only part that matters now is the bit that concerned me, Stanno and Micky Cullen. Stan and Micky were the closest friends I had, and we were an inseparable trio. Stan and I felt pretty much as the rest of the unit did about Captain Anscudden's exploits, but Micky was even more affected. After one particularly gruesome interrogation during which an Adeni youth's dying screams were punctuated by questions in that soft, expensive voice, Micky wrote a letter to Amnesty International detailing Anscudden's behavior and citing incidents and dates. Somehow the letter was intercepted and traced to Micky, although it was typed and unsigned. But instead of instituting court-martial proceedings against him, Anscudden decided to use his own methods. From that moment, the value of Micky's life fell to zero.

Anscudden finally got him in a Live Training Accident—an LTA. Really, there was never any need for such an extreme, because in any highly disciplined hierarchy like the British Army there's plenty of opportunity for neutralizing threats from the lower ranks in a legal, although not necessarily legitimate, manner. However, Captain Anscudden wanted his pound of flesh. Exactly how he arranged to get it was never discovered, but one day we launched a practice attack with air support on a deserted Arab village outside Shuqra. When it was all over, we were sent in to comb the ruins for "survivors." All we found was Micky Cullen. His left arm and leg were missing and his right foot was under the rubble of a collapsed Arab house, but he was recognizable, and all we knew was that he shouldn't have been there.

Stanno and I realized instantly that Anscudden had arranged it, but how he had done it and how we could prove it we never could work out. There was an inquiry, of course, but the official verdict of Accident laid the blame for his own death on Micky. His squad had been painting aiming marks on the flat roofs with red paint, but the area had been reported cleared an hour before the attack and it was thought everyone had been accounted for. However, although Micky's mates were certain he had left the village with the rest of them, no one could actually swear to having seen him do so.

From then on, Stanno and I were at war with Anscudden. There was little hope of success, though, and eventually I just wished he would simply stop existing—that the world would suddenly be free of Anscudden. But fate kept us together far beyond the point of discomfort. Part of the trouble was that the ex-captain of shooting was also a weapons man, and two years later we found ourselves helping to demonstrate new arms to foreign buyers in order to boost the export drive. Normally, an officer could arrange the transfer of a man he particularly disliked working with, but I was an expert and necessary. I used to see him at most of the demonstrations: Salisbury Plain, Essex marshes, Cumberland . . . A major now, he would chat quietly with a small group of men in continental mackintoshes and soft Eurocrat hats while I fired off a few bursts from the latest modification of the L7A1 machine gun: say, the L19A1 with the eight-pound barrel and other goodies. Then he'd wave a gloved hand at me and demonstrate how easy it was to interchange parts or fit the Enfield tripod, and I would give it a quick field strip. It always seemed to be raining, and there would be the aero-engine noises of military hovercraft being put through their paces by cocky foreign officers.

After a while I began to recognize a few regular customers with whom Anscudden was clearly on friendly terms. I'd look up, fingers numb with cold, to explain apologetically that the sodding gas regulator was faulty and see him in the middle of a huddle, their backs turned in a semicircle to me, collars up against the wind that came whipping across the ranges from the North Sea. A silver hip flask covered in pigskin would appear and circulate, the light would go and brant geese start honking in the distance.

I suppose I'd finally fallen out of love with the Army over the Micky Cullen affair. The way it conspired to hide its own skeletons no longer seemed a form of loyalty, and the way it allowed bastards like Anscudden to rise and prosper showed that the system I'd so admired had a flaw I wasn't prepared to live with. I was also pretty cheesed off with demonstrating small arms to toffee-nosed foreign officers. I pulled out in early 1970 and three weeks later heard that Anscudden had resigned his commission in favor of private enterprise. People do.

5

I was in the Javits Corporation office off Haymarket the following day when Moleman phoned to tell me that Selby was in the shop.

"He's very brown," said Moleman. "And he wants to see you somewhere where you can talk."

"It had better be there," I said, "and you can go home. This place"—I glanced behind me to see the secretary chatting up the man who had called to fix the document shredder—"is rather busy at the moment. Tell him I'll be right over."

Selby was ten years older than me and about fifteen years soberer. At about the time when I'd first watched avidly as the Buffs marched up and down the Scotland Hills, Selby had been called up for National Service and sent off to Kenya. He had left an officer and a gentleman and, being a born entrepreneur, had joined British Petroleum, thereafter moving pretty much in the oil crowd for as long as he could stand it.

"Dull buggers," he had said to me when we first met. It was in Singapore two years previously, when he'd been involved in negotiations for one of the concessions in the

Gulf of Siam. "They actually like the stuff, you know. It's black and it's smelly and it drives them wild with excitement. For me, oil means politics. . . . I wonder what one could possibly do with five thousand M-16s?"

"Captured?"

"Stolen. Brand new, the lot of them. They're now the property of Huu Siew Van."

"The minister?"

"Himself," Selby had nodded. "I've seen the guns. He's got them stacked in his private garage in Saigon."

"I think I could help you out," I said cautiously. "Do you know if his supply line can be kept live for long?"

"I don't know, but I can find out. What do you want?"

"Eighty-one-millimeter mortar bombs."

"U.S. or Soviet?" he asked. Thus our relationship started. It was true that weapons to me were what oil was to the dull buggers he had singled out for disparagement. Nevertheless, we had done a fair amount of business together.

Selby's own job was difficult to define, but he now acted as a sort of mediator between the Libyan Government and the international oil companies for whose revenues they were eager. Clearly it required skill, for each new incident in the Middle East produced tensions which painfully showed up the ambivalence of the Libyan position. It was not a simple matter of acknowledging national pride and the ignominy of having foreign companies exploit natural assets. That came into it; but so did the more purely political strains set up by pressure from the heads of the states that Gaddafi dreamed would solidify into a pan-Arab union and from the governments of the Western capitalist countries whose oil companies were so heavily committed.

Selby had friends in both camps and had been around long enough to get himself trusted, so he was a valuable man despite, or perhaps because of, having no official position. In short, he was an older man worldly enough to treat the world with the nonchalance and contempt to which I aspired. I also trusted him more than anyone other than Stanno and Micky Cullen. That's the good thing about officers and gentlemen: the real ones are like Selby, whereas the bogus ones are like Anscudden. Personal loyalty means something to the genuine article.

I found him in Lee & Savernake chatting to Moleman with one of my American gun-buff magazines open on his lap. I just hope Mole felt as self-conscious as I did that beside Selby's deep son-of-the-desert tan we looked a bit pallid.

"My wife'll be thinking I've got the sack if you keep sending me home in the middle of the day," said Moleman. "Now, you see, I'll have to eat my bloody sandwiches on a bench in Lincoln's Inn Fields." I locked the shop door behind his disgruntled back and pulled the blind down. Then I got the Scotch out from under the counter.

"Drink," said Selby; "that's what I need. It's getting to be as scarce as snow in Libya."

"Dry?" I asked.

"As the desert," said Selby. "I remember it being fairly relaxed under old King Idris; a lot of the estates used to produce their own wine. But now that Gaddafi has sent all the Italians back and declared a new Islam, you have to be damn careful about where you do your drinking. Assuming you can get the stuff in the first place." He took a long gulp of Scotch.

"You wanted to talk," I said.

37

"Right, Lee. I've come across some information that could be of value to you, not least because it concerns your employer."

"Javits?"

"Javits," echoed Selby. "Anyway, decide for yourself. In two weeks' time, a small freighter registered in Panama and named the *Trebizond* is due to leave Trieste. It's heading for Dar-es-Salaam. Does this ring any bells?"

I shook my head. "None," I said.

"Well, it's Javits' latest deal, and personally I'm not surprised he's kept his mouth shut, even to trusted employees." He smiled ironically. "On board the *Trebizond* will be, amongst other things, two thousand assault rifles and a hundred million rounds of seven-point-six-two-millimeter ammunition. In other words, fifty thousand rounds per weapon."

"Seven point six two?" I queried. "What are they? FNs?"

"No, Russian AKs. The ammunition is in boxes marked 'China clay—store away from heat,' and the guns are described as school laboratory equipment. Plus some pistols and a few bazookas. All in all, about sixteen million dollars' worth. Tanzania wants it, and it looks as though the CIA are putting up the money."

"Let me get this straight," I said. "The CIA are giving *Tanzania* money to buy arms from the Soviets?"

"Right. A nice irony, that. It's all on account of the need to be discreet. That's why the Tanzanian Government didn't go to the open market. With the present situation, no other government wants to declare partiality by supplying them, and private dealers like Interarms are too big to guarantee secrecy. Sam Cummings has agents everywhere, and the trade watches them like hawks, as you know. Probably one of the Hamburg toy shops could oblige, but it's simpler for the Tanzanians to buy indirectly through the agency from a discreet source."

"Nobody tells me anything," I said.

"Believe me, Lee, damn few people know about this one. Or at least, they didn't until a couple of days ago. That's why I'm here: somewhere there's been a leak and the Libyans have found out about Javits' shipment. It's got them really interested, partly because they don't want Tanzania to get more arms. Tanzania has close connections with Israel on the one hand, and on the other the Libyans supported Uganda in the limited war with Tanzania before the Mogadishu Agreement. So that's one good reason for intercepting the *Trebizond*. But the best reason is that the Libyans would like the arms themselves."

"What for?" I asked. "They must have masses of guns, with all their money."

"Quite," agreed Selby; "but they want weapons that can't easily be traced back to them. They want clean stuff because they're going to supply the rebels in northern Chad."

"Who are largely Semitic," I said, beginning to see.

"Exactly. They mostly speak Arabic or Sudanic dialects, and even if Gaddafi doesn't see them as fitting precisely into his pan-Arab world, at least they're Moslems and not a lot of Catholic blacks, who he thinks keep the southern half of Chad running as part of the French empire. Politics being what they are, it wouldn't be too clever of the Libyans openly to supply the rebels with arms for use against the French—mostly because Gaddafi is still hoping that the French will send him the Mirage fighters he ordered some while back."

"So the Libyans will try to nick Javits' shipment?" I asked.

"Because they don't want it to get to Dar and because they want the toys themselves."

"They plan to hijack it somewhere in the Mediterranean."

"Jesus," I said, refilling our glasses with Scotch. "How did you find all this out?"

"I have a friend in the Ministry of Foreign Defense," said Selby diffidently. "Well, he's the Minister, actually. Hamid Akrimi, Libyan Minister of Foreign Defense."

"Whatever that may mean," I said.

"It makes more sense than it sounds if you remember Libya's ambition to constitute a fresh rallying point in the Arab world. Mutual-defense pacts, all that."

"Is he reliable?"

"He's reliable," said Selby.

"So why are you telling me this?" I asked.

"Well," said Selby, "seeing as how you work for Javits and seeing as how you're always short of £SD, I thought you could maybe earn a bit by going to Javits like the faithful employee that you are and telling him you've found out that Tanzania isn't the only place interested in his shipment. Tell him you know the Libyans are planning to steal the *Trebizond*. That should make him pretty grateful, I'd think. I reckon you could reasonably ask for a bonus on the strength of it. I mean, he ought to pay a lot to find out when and where somebody is plotting to steal sixteen million bucks' worth of armaments from him."

"It's a thought," I said tentatively.

"Moreover," went on Selby, "a really bright Corporation man might well volunteer to help foil the attempt. For a further consideration, of course."

"Oh, come on," I protested. "I'm no heavy, and Javits

knows it. He employed me because I know about firearms, not because I've got muscles in the head."

"You've been around," said Selby. "You can look after yourself, Lee. If I know your record in Aden, you can be sure Javits does. In any case, he'll be thankful to keep the whole thing within the Corporation. But if you still don't like the idea as it stands, maybe I can add some inducement."

"Like more money, for instance?"

"Lots more money," nodded Selby. "Sixteen million bucks, to be precise. We're going to nick that ship ourselves."

There was a short silence while I tried to think of something to say.

"Just let me get this straight," I said finally. "You propose to steal a Panamanian freighter and sixteen million dollars' worth of arms paid for by the CIA? Just take it away from Javits and two governments with stakes in it?"

"Why not?" Selby wanted to know. "You can hardly have anything against stealing from your own employer: you've been doing it for the last three years. Only this time you'll never need to work again. You can retire for life."

"But how will you work it, for God's sake? You and whose army?"

"Just you and me."

"You're nuts," I told him. "It's all that sun. Maybe you've got what the Foreign Legion used to call *le cafard*."

Selby reached out a brown hand and poured himself another drink.

"Just listen," he said. "At least give me credit for having done my bloody homework, Lee. None of it's as difficult as you think, because I know exactly what the Libyan end of

41

the plan is. They propose to put a team aboard the *Trebizond* right from the start, in Trieste. Somewhere around the foot of Italy they'll take the ship over and make straight for Tripoli, probably picking up a Libyan Navy escort after they've passed Malta. All we have to do is stop them taking over the ship and hijack it ourselves. Then we'll drive the thing off to a quiet place I know and unload it before anyone's the wiser. I've got it all worked out. I don't make mistakes, Lee; especially not when my own retirement's also at stake."

I swirled Scotch around my glass thoughtfully. I had to admit that the idea did have an elemental simplicity. I stood to lose my job, of course, but by then I would have picked up a bonus from Javits plus extra pay for protecting his cargo and finally half the value of the cargo itself.

"How do you propose to get aboard the *Trebizond*?" I asked. Lee smiled.

"We may resort to that old gag and sit in a rubber dinghy pretending to be shipwrecked yachtsmen, firing off rockets and calling weakly for help on little radios. It's irresistible."

I mulled it over some more.

"Fifty-fifty?" I asked at length.

"That's what I thought."

"Hm. I think we'll need help. Two of us makes bad odds. We could use another man."

"If you insist," said Selby. "But your share goes down. Whom did you have in mind?"

"Stanno. He's with the Army in Northern Ireland at the moment, and he wants out. There isn't much he doesn't know about the rough stuff. How about if you take forty percent and Stan and I split the sixty between us?"

"Okay," said Selby after a moment's thought. "I admit the chances are better with three."

"That leaves us with one question," I said. "Whom are we up against? Who've the Libyans hired to snatch the boat?"

"A guy called Anscudden."

"Jesus H."

"Right," nodded Selby. "Your man. That's the clincher."

When the surprise had partially worn off, I said: "You don't imagine that a gent like Anscudden would stoop to anything as low as leading a gang of pirates over the rail of a merchantman, do you? He's an awfficer, and awfficers don't get their hands dirty—partly because it goes against the grain, but mostly because they might get caught. But in any case, why should he? How's he being paid?"

"Half now, half on delivery. Cash now and the rest as he likes when he gets to Tripoli. Into a numbered account, if he wants. The Libyans don't care; they'll pay him in diamonds if that's what he says. They just want that boat."

"How the hell did he get in with the Libyans in the first place?" I asked.

"Old school tie-ups," said Selby. "Much as you'd expect. My Minister friend Akrimi's an officer, ex-Sandhurst, and he's known Anscudden for years. Anscudden is in the business and keeps both ears to the ground . . ."

"Simultaneously, if I know that bastard," I said. Selby grinned.

"No, left and right alternately. He's generously prepared to overlook ideological differences if it's a question of money. When Hamid got wind of this shipment to Tanzania he was dead interested, and so was Gaddafi, especially as he couldn't see anything in it to contravene his religious principles. A chance for Moslem solidarity, no less; so he's prepared to pay friend Anscudden one hundred and fifty thousand dollars for that ship, and he doesn't care how Anscudden does it so long as it doesn't make the headlines."

"So," I said, "with his initial seventy-five grand he can round up a small crew to do the nasty work for him. Then I presume he'll fly down to Tripoli as the boat steams in and pick up the rest from your mate Hamid. Smiles all round and tough shit on the Tanzanians."

"That's about it," agreed Selby.

The news that Anscudden was involved had finally decided me. I reasoned that nothing would drop Anscudden so effectively in the shit as having the *Trebizond* steam into Tripoli harbor with not a gun on board while he stood on the quay grinning confidently. Here was a golden opportunity to square a long-standing feud. Not that I was motivated by a merely vulgar sense of revenge. I did indeed hate him, but it was not the insane hatred that officers sometimes like to inspire in their subordinate victims, knowing their caste makes them safe. Far from doing anything foolish, I was about to demonstrate how Anscudden's careless manipulation of his class and rank had at last left him vulnerable. I was also about to make a good deal of money.

"Javits will be good and mad," I said at length.

"I thought he already was," said Selby. "I don't know anybody in the trade who doesn't think your employer's round the twist. Sorry to have to tell you."

"Old Javits is no more than slightly eccentric," I maintained stoutly.

"To be slightly eccentric in the armaments business is to be insane," said Selby. "How about that deal you arranged for him in Hamburg, supplying the Basque nationalists?"

I was startled. "How did you hear about that?" I demanded.

"Well, it became common knowledge, didn't it? An already tricky delivery problem, and the first case of weapons smuggled in to the poor bloody Basques contains ten gross Christmas crackers from the Kaufhof and a printed note saying, 'Thou shalt not kill.' Your man's screwy," said Selby decisively. "You'll be well out of the Javits Corporation."

"Okay," I said. "Let's set about getting there. I'll meet you in Vienna after I've seen Javits."

6

There was some rapid spadework to be done before I was able two days later to send a registered letter to Stanno in Londonderry enclosing a civilian passport. The passport was Swedish and had cost me two hundred dollars; but if you're going to desert from the Army, it's as well to vanish completely for a year or two. After that the memory fades and you're safe, barring getting caught speeding or rate-paying. I told him to meet me in Brussels as soon as possible.

I left the post office with little to do except wait for my late-afternoon flight to Vienna. I'd already phoned Javits the day before to let him know I was coming. Ringing Javits was never much fun, because he was convinced that the Austrians were tapping his phone, but this time he had been so maniacally cautious he refused even to believe I was who I said I was. It's a fine thing when your own boss won't recognize you. After dialing code numbers involving about twenty digits, I heard distant ringing. Then a voice.

"Javits," it said in an all-purpose American accent.

"Lee McGundrell here, Mr. Javits. I've just learned something that is going to affect you shortly. When can we meet?"

There was a brief silence. Very faintly on another line somewhere, a voice was speaking German.

"Not good enough, Mr. Lee," said Javits. "I'm a busy man and I sure as hell don't waste my time on oddballs making threats."

"This isn't a threat," I assured him.

"Where are you calling from?"

"London."

"Well, Mr. Lee in London, I don't know what you want, but if you'd like to pop over to Vienna and tell me about it, I might just give you a cup of coffee. I'm afraid you'll have to buy your own plane ticket."

"It won't cost you a thing, Mr. Javits," I said. "I even like it black with no sugar."

There was a sudden increase in volume on the line.

"Hey-hey," came his voice, now full of amiability, "that's my boy okay. Hi there, Lee. Nobody else in the whole wide world drinks their goddam coffee like that. Sure, just turn up any time. Oh—and Lee?"

"Yuh?" I said faintly.

"I was kidding you about the ticket."

"I knew that, Mr. Javits. It's just that I wasn't letting on."

Now as I walked back home, Blackheath was a flat expanse crisscrossed with distant lines of traffic and dotted with knots of boys playing football. But I was immune to the freezing wind that blew up from Greenwich, because I was warmed from within by the knowledge that at last I was going to break Anscudden in the name of Micky Cullen and a lot of unsung Adenis, who in any case now had their independence.

A football rolled towards me, a group of boys thirty yards away looking impatiently in my direction. I gave it a hefty boot and then made a feeble gesture of apology or appeasement as the ball shot off at a tangent, ending up just as far from the game as when I had kicked it. I never could get the damn things to go where I wanted.

Once home, I grabbed an early lunch, checked on the time of takeoff and put a few essentials into a briefcase. I debated taking my gun, but decided it was better left wrapped in its oiled silk under the tiled fireplace. There was no point in running the risk of being frisked at the airport by somebody who knew his job: they surely couldn't all be as inexperienced as the last three who had checked me through the barriers. In any case, where I was going I could choose practically any weapon I needed. Nevertheless, I was sorry, because like most people who like guns, I felt incomplete without my own. I suppose you could if you wished make out a case for my being haunted by feelings of inadequacy or sexual impotence or something, which is fine by me; but all I should like to say is that I'm fond of this gun because it has been with me for some time and is a relatively uncommon *marque* for a personal weapon.

It was bequeathed me by an Israeli friend who'd died of food poisoning in Malta. He was a nice guy, and it was a pretty ignominious way for a good professional to go. Practically the last lucid thing he said was for me to take care that not too much was left around to make for awkward questions. It was rather touching, considering he was staying in a dismal hotel in Valletta with a toothbrush, a nondescript passport, two hundred ninety-seven dollars in cash and a Czech Model 52 pistol. The cash paid for his bill and a quiet burial, but I kept the gun because it was a beauty. Although it was the current Czech service pistol, somebody along the line had had the barrel engraved with a few light curlicues, and the result was a slightly dressy but potent handgun. It's an original design, not just another foreign-made Browning, except that its locking system is the same as that of the German MG-42 machine gun. It isn't particularly small, being eight and a quarter inches long, but with more than four and a half inches of barrel, it's a lot more accurate than most of those Walthers and Berettas. The only drawback is that the ideal ammunition is less easy to come by than certain other types. So it's necessary to keep tabs on a supply of Russian or Czech ammunition for this pistol—preferably Czech, because their loads are something like twenty percent heavier even than the Russian and can give you a velocity of around sixteen hundred feet per second. Once or twice when I've really been scared, I've taken the military bullets out of the Czech cartridge and substituted half-jacketed hollow-points and even wadcutters. Wadcutters have the aerodynamics of a can of baked beans, but provided you don't want long-range performance, they're a powerful argument. They knock great chunks of meat out, and I've never seen anybody get up and ask for more. You can do a lot of damage with one, and the magazine holds eight rounds.

I tucked the gun regretfully away again, put back the fireplace tiles and washed my hands. Then I set off to catch the five forty-five BEA flight to Vienna.

Security at London Airport is a bit of a farce, despite much-vaunted stringent methods to prevent hijackings and what the press calls "bomb outrages." It isn't too difficult to bring stuff into the country: eighteen months ago I walked in with a couple of AK-47 assault rifles thinly disguised as golf clubs. The essential thing is an onward flight to somewhere, so that when you land at Heathrow you can go into the Transit Lounge. There, you wander about until you blend into the background before going purposefully through the plain door to the left of the bar. This will get you out into the catering section via a large mop cupboard. Turn right and keep walking as if looking for somebody. If stopped, ask if they've seen John or Mr. Cartwright because you've got a piece of baggage that's gone astray. You heft the golf bag. Ten to one they'll think you're Baggage Link or Security and direct you out of their section into the main Arrivals Hall, where you get the hell out into the light rain that's falling.

The reverse procedure needs planning and is slightly trickier. As for a personal search that particular afternoon, I certainly could have been draped with armaments for all the men at the barrier knew. Someday someone will have to tell them that if they've overcome their natural British squeamishness to the extent of running their hands up the inside of a complete stranger's leg, then they can take the plunge and feel the small of his back, hip pockets, upper rear calf, back of neck and inner arm. You'd be surprised how easy it is to lose a knife or a compact handgun. I've known Orthodox Jews to climb aboard a Trident with little Colt .25 autos taped up into the crowns of their hats, which is just about the first damn place I would look—but then, I'm not much overawed by religion.

7

It was a nice flat off Königstrasse, if you like flats with black carpets throughout and white furniture. Either way, it was a far cry from Jubilee Terrace—not least in respect of the heavy in the foyer and faithful Frick, who met me as I stepped out of the lift and frisked me expertly and apologetically before showing me into Javits' front room. The noise of traffic in the busy street below was muffled by double glazing. It came through like the distant sound of surf.

Javits bounced in and greeted me as affably as he'd ever done, while Frick faded away in the background.

"I'm sorry about the fuck-up on the phone, Lee," he said. "Fact is, you can't be too careful."

"Damn right," I agreed. "It's leaks I've come to talk about."

The head of the Javits Corporation was impressively ugly, even once one had got over the shock of meeting an albino black. Nothing about him looked natural. His skin was not pale so much as colorless, a dead white as if he had been blanched, but with here and there brown flecks of pigmentation like grave marks on the backs of his hands. Even the thin scrub of gingerish hair receding up his white forehead looked wiry and disconnected, the way the cheaper wigs do.

I'd seen pubic hair with that texture and hadn't liked it much then.

A girl in a dirndl skirt wheeled in some coffee.

"No sugar, no cream, Lee. Right?" asked Javits, grinning. "How's business in the U.K.?" he asked as the girl poured coffee.

"Yours or mine?"

Javits laughed, and there was an awkward pause as I took the cup and the girl went out. "Leaks, you say?" he went on. "Such as?"

"Such as on Wednesday week—in other words, nine days' time—you have a freighter named *Trebizond* on charter to sail from Trieste with a cargo destined for Tanzania. That much has leaked, for a start. But I also know there's a plan afoot to hijack your shipment. I thought you might like to hear about the when and the where. And the who."

Javits had put his cup down gently. His face had closed, and his voice sounded as it had over the telephone.

"What was the ship called again?" he asked.

"This could get boring," I said. Javits sighed and rolled his pinkish eyes.

"Well, Lee. Let's suppose for the sake of argument that I do have such a ship under charter and that it does have a cargo aboard which someone might want to steal. What makes you think I'm incapable of making my own security arrangements to ensure its safe arrival? We do quite a lot of shipping in our line of business, don't we? As you know, the Corporation's not in the habit of losing its consignments."

"Then we don't want to break the record by losing this one, do we?"

"Hell no. But anyway, there's always insurance if the worst should happen."

"Not in this case, Mr. Javits; I doubt that very much. I don't think you'd be able to get this cargo insured. Not unless it was just innocuous stuff like, for instance, china clay or school lab equipment."

Javits sighed, but it was more a sign of acknowledgment than a gesture of resignation.

"Okay," he said, "word's got out. That's bad, Lee. Believe me, I'm very grateful to you for letting me know in time."

"Hell, I work for the company, Mr. Javits," I said smugly. "I keep my ear to the ground. It's in both our interests."

"Sure," he said. "Know any more?"

"Bits and pieces."

"It'd be worth a couple of thousand of your pounds to me. Plus that air fare, of course. A fully justified bonus for good work."

I grinned. "That's pretty generous of you, Mr. Javits," I said. "I'd also like to know where the leak was. All I do know is that somehow or other the Libyans have got wind of the Tanzania deal. They don't like that a bit, and they can use the toys themselves, so they've hired somebody to divert your ship. I only heard this because I've got a good friend on the ground in Tripoli."

Javits had got to his feet and was staring down into Königstrasse through the double glazing.

"I had hoped this was one deal that wouldn't become a subject of gossip," he said bitterly at the distant traffic. "But since it has, congratulations on being so well informed, in addition to being an expert in your own field. Now, as a loyal member of the Corporation, what would you suggest to protect our interests, huh? Tell me that."

I suppose it took me about ten minutes to convince him that he should pay me to do the job myself. He liked the idea of keeping it in the family, but was less keen when I mentioned bringing Stanno and Selby in. I couldn't blame him. The idea of giving even a minimum of Company information away to outsiders, and one of them a deserter at that, worried Javits quite a bit. But in any case, he'd have had to hire strangers, and I still had my job with the Corporation to bargain with. I undertook to guarantee my friends' silence and reliability. I also undertook to guarantee the safety of the *Trebizond*'s cargo myself. I was only sorry that I couldn't point out the irony of that to Javits.

"It's a hell of a lot of money you're asking for," he growled eventually.

"A hundred thousand dollars?" I said. "It's not much. It's peanuts for safeguarding you against the loss of sixteen millions' worth of someone else's military hardware. Anyway, I'll only be getting sixty grand: the other forty gets split between my mates."

Not long after he had agreed to this, Javits began making suggestions of his own, such as that the Corporation had warehousing facilities on Malta where the *Trebizond* could be unloaded and the arms transferred to another ship for their journey to Dar-es-Salaam. By that time, he said, the Libyans' hijacking attempt should have taken place and been foiled, but the *Trebizond* would have become hot.

"As a matter of fact, I've got some things we can put aboard in Malta which can then go on to Tripoli," said Javits. "After all, it would never do to have the ship arriving without a stick on board. I've got just the job."

"What?" I asked.

Javits smiled. His teeth were perfectly white and even, which always came as a surprise. "Those two thousand old Lee-Enfields that Libya put on the market not six months

54

ago," he said. "They can have them back. At least they'll
know how to fire *them*."

Javits had just finished clearing up delivery details with
the Soviets. Apparently the weapons due for Tanzania were
not the Russian AKs that Selby had thought, but Czech
Model 58 assault rifles. These look very much like the AK
and fire the same Soviet rimless cartridge, but the weapons
have internal differences. Nevertheless, it was a shrewd
selection by the Tanzanians, assuming that they had chosen
rather than had the choice made for them by their friendly
local Comecon salesman.

Javits had a sample of their wares in his apartment, and
I thought it was a nice job except for the weight. The
Czech weapon is anyway about two pounds lighter than the
Russian, but this particular rifle was lighter still because it
was fitted with a plastic stock and handguards. I doubted
if, even when loaded, it would have weighed eight pounds
compared, for example, with the loaded weight of nearly
ten and a half pounds of the British version of the FN. This
sounds ideal, of course, but I saw a drawback. With full-
or semiautomatic shoulder weapons, a saving in weight is
not necessarily a great advantage, because of the tendency
of the muzzle to rise during automatic fire. With a round as
small as 7.62mm it's easy to miss a target in any case, and
if you miss your target on full-auto fire at a cyclic rate of
between seven hundred and eight hundred rounds per minute, you can burn up an awful lot of ammunition without
much show for it except earache.

Javits had arranged to accept the consignment in Trieste.
Although the goods coming from Prague would arrive by
rail marked as china clay and chemical apparatus, the

Soviets were still supplying him with efficient documenta-
tion, including end-use certificates, in case the Italians
started opening the crates. End-use certificates, traditionally
signed by ambassadors or recognizably senior government
officials, are to a consignment of arms what an onward-
journey ticket is to a traveler in a country with strict immigration controls. Most European countries are unwilling to
allow arms to cross their borders, even in transit, without
some indication, if not firm proof, that their destination has
been officially sanctioned. In this case, I didn't doubt that
the end-use documents the Soviets gave Javits would have
the signature of a Tanzanian minister on them together
with the country's seal, if not President Nyerere's autograph.

8

Selby arrived in Vienna early next morning. I told him that Javits was in the know and the whole thing was fixed.

"I'll introduce you before I go to collect Stan," I said. "Just to convince him you're a gentleman." At the time, of course, I didn't realize quite what a joke that was.

"What do you think?" Selby asked me as we walked down Domgasse. "Will Anscudden use pros or roughnecks?"

"I don't know," I said. The ex-major no longer had a platoon at his beck and call. "Pros come expensive, and they're harder to find at short notice. On the other hand, there's no shortage of thugs for hire. I reckon he'll need four or five: perhaps one pro, or someone who knows enough to make sure the captain sets the right course for Tripoli, and the rest can be hired hands to keep the crew in order. He'll want to keep costs down to maximize profits, as they say."

"Where'll he do his shopping?"

"If I were Anscudden, I'd put it out over the grapevine that I needed a good man in a hurry. If I found him quick enough, I'd let him get his own team together; otherwise I'd just round up a few down in Trieste. There are plenty of kids in a port who wouldn't mind a couple of days' piracy in exchange for some quick lire."

We went to a bar I knew in Schlachtgasse. Warty old Krause was still there, ministering sourly to a handful of early drinkers who were sitting miserably in front of glasses that probably contained Fernet Branca, and serve them right.

"*Du liebe Zeit,*" he said on catching sight of me, a well-rehearsed look of startled pleasure on his face. "Herr Lee. What a happiness. And friend. Gentlemen." He thrust out a hand knobbly with warts. I nodded.

"Hello, Krause," I said. "Back in merry old Wien. I didn't come here to see you, so don't bother to look hurt and disappointed. I want to use your phone. Perhaps you'd fix my friend up with drinks and things while I do so?" I put some schillings down on the bar.

"Why, certainly, certainly." Krause beamed and draped a white cloth over one forearm. You couldn't dent the bugger, and God knew I'd tried.

I called a couple of people in Brussels and one in Frankfurt. Then, as an afterthought, I tried a man about ten blocks away who ran a lucrative but legitimate business converting surplus military arms into beautifully finished sporting weapons. Checkered walnut stocks, scope sights and all. At the end of twenty minutes, I had gathered some information.

"He's got Brückner," I told Selby, sitting down at the table. He was flicking through some pornographic magazines which Krause supplied to good customers who looked as though they'd run out of things to say to each other.

"Who's Brückner?" he asked, not looking up from a copy of *Dog Instruction No. 4.*

"He's good," I said. "He was in that Sofia affair in '71. You remember, the morphine-for-guns deal that went sour when they were shopped by the coachbuilder who put the compartments into their Mercedes. He also helped Oerlikon supply Israel *and* Egypt before the Six-Day War. That's his strength: Brückner doesn't specialize, and neither does he stand on his dignity. He'll do large jobs and small ones, but whatever he does he does well. Anscudden was lucky to find him at such short notice. I rang Mariot in Brussels, and he said he'd heard Anscudden had gone on the market for one man only. Nobody knows what it's for or where, so at least he's being discreet."

"It looks as though you were right, Lee," said Selby. "Jesus," he added with disgust, throwing down his copy of *Schoolroom Sex,* which featured boys and girls not much over the age of twenty-nine, "I wish I'd been approached by one of these Danish studios when I was at school. I'd have done it for free—all those chicks in gym slips."

"Judging by what you're reading, it's probably still not too late to put your name down," I said. Selby shook his head sadly.

"It wouldn't be the same," he said. "I wouldn't enjoy it now. I've been hardened and corrupted."

"Then you're just the man to go after Brückner."

"Look, maybe he *is* good," said Selby, "but he'll still be relying on a bunch of waterfront heavies to provide the muscle."

"Nevertheless, it needs careful planning," I said. "We can't be certain that Anscudden will end up doing what he told the Libyans he was going to do. He may tell Brückner to infiltrate the *Trebizond's* crew right from the start, or he may decide to hold up the ship anywhere between the

Adriatic and Sicily. Meanwhile, I'll see if I can get you a lift down to Trieste with Javits. We're going to need equipment, and he'll have access to it even if he hasn't got it in stock." I glanced at my watch. "Why don't I take you over to meet Javits now?"

Selby looked at me. "Why not?" he said, and he smiled. They were the second-whitest teeth I'd seen in two days.

I left Selby in Vienna and flew back to fetch Stanno from Brussels, where I checked in at the friendly old Vendôme near the Rue de Char et Pain. I wondered how long I would have to wait. Stan had probably skipped already and might be on his way to Dublin.

I took myself off for a bite. It was one way of killing time. On the way I passed the nightclub that used to be called the Gun Bourse but which has been abandoned by our crowd ever since a succession of cub reporters and television documentary-makers identified it and started asking people if they worked for Sam Cummings or if they had ever flown "Mauser toys" into the Congo. The club has now been entirely taken over by journalists all trying to pretend that because they can remember the cyclic rate of fire of the FAL they have strong connections with the world of international arms dealing. One or two of them know something, but they keep quiet. In any case, they have silently followed the big people to Hamburg, where the conversation is uniformly boring because they're just businessmen at heart, assuming they have such things.

I ate frugally and read a Belgian newspaper. I admit to being a self-educated man, and I'm neither proud nor defensive about it. I'm interested in knowledge because I don't like being conned, and I'm interested in increasing my word power because it might even help me to con others in an emergency. I read a column or two about Libya sending military hardware to General Amin in Uganda, but as I was relying on more than AP reports, I probably knew more about it than the journalist did. I abandoned the paper for *The Agony and the Ecstasy*. I was pleased to see I had only another four-hundred-odd pages to go. I hate eating alone.

Stanno turned up at eleven the next morning. A thin, unfriendly face in its mid-twenties appeared in the foyer, and he followed me upstairs and dumped a Sainsbury's carrier bag on my bed.

"Glad you're here, Stan," I said. "Problems?"

"Nope." He shook his head. "They'll go on thinking I've been knocked off by the Provos for a couple more days; then when nobody talks, I'll be posted missing, believed AWOL."

"No hero's death?"

"Not in Northern Ireland, at any rate. But I've got a nasty prickly feeling between the shoulder blades."

"That's only what Moleman calls scarperer's itch. Don't worry, I've got a cure for it."

"Like money?" He rummaged in the carrier bag and produced a bottle of duty-free Haig. "Care for a drink?"

I nodded, and he made two Scotch-and-waters in the Duralex glasses that hotels believe people need for cleaning their teeth.

"Cheers," he said. His face was very pale, the skin taut with the strain of the last few days. Even so, it was recognizably the same face of the serious boy with reddish springy hair whose friendship had meant a lot to me out in Aden a few years ago, both before and after Micky Cullen's death. Stan was a Liverpudlian with a father who had come from Poland or Czechoslovakia or somewhere during the war.

From the first, I'd noticed the professional attitude he took to soldiering. It was neither the ingratiating eagerness shown by those who wanted careers, nor was it the dour skiving of those who merely desired to escape their social circumstances. Rather, Stanno had shown that he needed the Army to stand as a sort of khaki bulwark against the needling insecurity and wastefulness of civilian life. In this rough shelter he had flourished, learned skills and become confident. Now it seemed he was old enough to do without the Army.

After I left, I suppose it was inevitable that we should have become less close. Nevertheless, the previous summer he had taken a fortnight's paid leave and joined me in Yugoslavia. He had brought a girl with him—a pretty and rather baffled creature from Lisburn named Sheilagh— whom he ignored most of the time except at night, when they would make violent love in a way that was audible throughout the Hotel Dubrovnik. Only somebody that unselfconscious could, at the end of ten days, have remained the only person in the building who didn't know that he habitually shouted, "Oh, God, I'm coming" about half an hour after going to bed. I don't think any of the Hotel Dubrovnik's guests really believed that it was a declaration of religious intention, and they couldn't keep their eyes off the fresh love bites that covered Stanno's neck at the breakfast table each morning.

I smiled at him and raised my glass. "So how's the old Army doing in its pitiless campaign against the tyrant and terrorist?"

"A real ball of fire. Same as ever; just like Aden. Baffled by politics. We're strong, simple working-class lads all aged eighteen who accept cups of tea from grateful natives in between doing an impossible job under intense provocation."

"Believed to be a reference to the M-1 carbine."

"No, those are called highly dangerous. Intense provocation means being spat at by women on both sides and called a motherfucker by children of five. Believe me, I'm glad to be out: I've had the Micks up to here. As far as I'm concerned, they can hack each other to ribbons."

"Ah, that's just the impartial noninvolvement one would expect from a Swedish national."

"I was forgetting I'm a foreigner," grinned Stanno. "Peder Beckers, indeed. But it's a nice passport all the same; thanks. How much?"

"Two fifty?" I suggested.

"Nope."

"Two hundred," I agreed. "I thought you might have got out of touch. I'll subtract it from your loot, shall I?"

"It's time you told me why the hell I'm here," said Stanno. "I don't mind defecting from the Army and becoming a wanted criminal; nor do I mind suddenly turning into a Swedish citizen. But I assume it's going to be worth it?"

"Your trust does you credit," I told him. "That's what armies are for. They inspire loyalty and comradeship."

"What about money?" Stanno wanted to know. "There's nothing wrong in being a paid comrade."

"True; although for us this caper's also going to be worth personal satisfaction in large quantities."

So I told him about the plan to steal the *Trebizond* for ourselves under the guise of protecting it for Javits, and his reaction was pretty much as mine had been.

"For fuck's sake," he said. "You must be nuts. God, I'm back off to Northern Ireland. You needn't bother to come to the airport."

63

"Under the circumstances, Mr. Beckers, it would make more sense if you headed for Stockholm."

"Oh, shit. I don't know anybody there."

He got up and went to the window, peering down into the streets of Brussels. A commercial jet roared overhead, and I caught a glimpse of a gray wing tip from where I sat on the bed.

"There is some icing," I added.

"What?"

I smiled. "Simply that the man the Libyans are paying to arrange their hijacking turns out to be a gent named Anscudden. Ex-Major T. Anscudden; school shooting ace, friend of the Irish Republican Army, hero of Aden and late of the Thanet Fusiliers. Now a free-lance munitions manipulator."

Stanno had turned away from the window in astonishment. "*Very* good," he said at length. "Oh, I like it a lot. How did you find that out?"

"I didn't," I admitted. "Selby did."

"Jesus Christ. That bastard Anscudden again. That makes a difference. You mean we'd be up against him?"

"In effect. He's hired a guy called Brückner to do his dirty work, but when we take the boat away from Brückner it's Anscudden we'll be dropping in the shit, because the Libyans will already have paid him hard cash to come up with the goods."

"Christ." He shook his head. "There're about a hundred things I don't understand, but one of them is why would Anscudden go along with stealing Javits' shipment? I thought they were supposed to be pally back in your own Army days. Out in Malaysia, wasn't it?"

"That's right, and as far as I know they still are as friendly as it's possible for two rivals in the same line of business to be. But the point is that Anscudden doesn't know this is Javits' deal. Because of the CIA involvement and because Javits is a cool worker at the best of times, he's presented what the Americans call a low profile. You know what the arms crowd are like—all gossip and rumor and treading on each other's faces at the first hint of a deal. No, Javits has kept very quiet about this. Anscudden will think that the agency have stage-managed everything for Tanzania, including the shipping arrangements."

From outside came the roar of a DC-8 coming in to land. They must have rerouted the flight paths since I was last in the Vendôme: it used to be almost a quiet hotel.

"We can make him look a complete arsehole," said Stanno enthusiastically. "The Libyans'll be mad and think he's a double-crosser, and the trade will get a laugh out of him for being outwitted. The only thing is," he added, "what happens to us? We'll be stuck with a load of Czech assault rifles belonging to the Tanzanians, or the CIA if you like. We'll still have to get rid of them to make the real money."

"Not satisfied with Javits' twenty thousand?"

"Let's say I'd be more satisfied with the jackpot."

"Selby's taking care of that part," I said.

"No offense, Lee, but you do trust him?"

"Totally. After it's been transferred in Malta, he'll take the stuff on to somewhere he knows. Then it'll be quietly faded."

"I only hope the same thing won't be happening to us," said Stanno.

9

At one o'clock on the Saturday morning, we were bobbing in a rubber dinghy thirty-two miles off Ancona, on the eastern coast of Italy. Half an hour previously, Javits had dropped us off the launch, having first made elaborate calculations involving wind speed, current and our probable drift, correlating these with the last position of the *Trebizond* as seen on the launch's radar. If he'd been right, the *Trebizond* should be no farther than ten miles away and closing fast. If he'd been wrong, or if the ship had since altered course, we might be sitting there for some days yet. Still, at least we'd be sitting there with money in our pockets, because Javits had already given me our fifty-thousand-dollar advance. The other half would come when we had delivered the *Trebizond* and its cargo safely to Malta.

The consignment had arrived from Prague on time, and Javits had seen it checked and stowed. He said there'd been no sign of Brückner, but according to the *Trebizond's* captain, four of his crew had left the ship suddenly on one pretext or another and he'd signed on their replacements himself. The captain was a Sri Lankan named Ratnayaka, who said that four new crew members at once was not particularly unusual, except that he could never remember anybody's having wanted to remain in Trieste before. There was, he intimated, no accounting for taste, and he added irrelevantly that on a previous voyage he'd been asked to perform a marriage ceremony for the bosun and the wireless operator, who had sworn to remain true to each other in the South China Sea.

It had struck all three of us that it would have been simpler had we also joined the *Trebizond* in Trieste, but Javits had had an answer to that one.

"This way there'll be a better chance of flushing out any of Brückner's men already aboard and of convincing Ratnayaka that you're on my side. The fact is," he said ruefully, "if I went and told him I'd put your lot aboard because I suspected some of his crew were hijackers, he'd have set his teeth like a goddam mule. I know that captain: he's good, but he's kind of temperamental. I just couldn't tell him he had two rival gangs aboard; he would simply have refused to sail."

Which was how we came to be wallowing in the Adriatic in pitch darkness. It seemed likely that the four new hands were Brückner's men, but it wasn't certain; either way, there was nothing to stop Brückner holding up the ship at a later stage with reinforcements.

"Shall I try the radio?" suggested Selby. Like Stanno and myself, he was wearing USAF survival gear. Although we were dry, we were shivering with cold.

"Give it another five minutes," I said. "She must be getting close, but there might be a fishing smack with radio that we missed on the radar. We'd look bloody idiots being picked up by a bunch of Italian fishermen and having to look grateful as they took us back to Ancona."

Javits' stock of equipment had indeed been comprehensive. In addition to the air/sea rescue kit, he had given us anything we asked for by way of personal weapons. We didn't need anything fancy: if there was to be any shooting, it would all be close-quarter work, and we needed something that could be concealed under our flying suits. Stanno had opted for a Sterling, a weapon he was familiar with. Selby chose a Ruger Blackhawk Special, a great cannon of a revolver taking a .44 magnum cartridge. As an example of the comprehensiveness of Javits' selection of ammunition, Selby had been given a box of a hundred reloaded cartridges in addition to the standard factory-loads and chose those in preference. They'd been put together by a gun enthusiast on the staff of the U.S. Embassy in Vienna before he'd been posted to Saigon, and according to the handwritten label on the box, they consisted of 210-grain jacketed hollow-point bullets backed by 29 grains of Hodgdon's H-110 pistol powder. Selby tried out this combination of gun and load in the hills behind Ancona, and we were all duly impressed and even slightly overawed by the weapon. It was probably the most potent handgun currently on the market. Selby later took a pencil and, estimating that we were getting a velocity of around 1700 feet per second, worked out that it signified a kinetic energy of something over 1300 foot-pounds, which, as Selby said, was damn near enough to sink the *Trebizond* if it refused to stop.

For myself I selected perhaps the nastiest gun in the world for close-up fighting: a riot gun. Riot guns are mostly nothing but sophisticated versions of the sawed-off shotgun, firing 12-gauge cartridges. However, the weapon I chose was the High Standard Model 10, which was developed in the U.S. primarily for police work. At first sight this weapon is unrecognizable as a shotgun, being only 26½ inches long with a curved butt plate instead of a stock. With a pistol-grip trigger assembly, it looks more like a submachine gun, and its action is, indeed, automatic. To go with it I picked a whole range of cartridges from standard 12-gauge buckshot loads through to BRI sabots. In effect, these are waisted bullets, and in a weapon with a reasonable barrel length they'll give a muzzle energy of 2200 foot-pounds. In other words, the sabot slug'll go happily through eighth-inch steel plate at a hundred yards with energy to spare and is accurate enough to give an eighteen-inch group at two hundred yards. It's no good pretending you can take cover from a gun like that: it can eat away anything short of a concrete bunker.

"Shall I put that call out now?" asked Selby again. I looked at my watch.

"Go ahead. We might as well switch on our jacket lights as well."

Selby began putting out a series of heartrending "May-day" calls on the short-range radio. Occasionally when we bobbed up on the swell I caught glimpses of navigation lights out across the black waste, but it was impossible to tell how far away they were. We pulled the inflation cords on our jackets, which also turned on the lights. I thought we'd been bloody fools to sit in a rubber dinghy at night with uninflated jackets round our necks, but they're so cumbersome, and anyway, they inflate automatically on immersion. Stanno uncovered the rescue light on the dinghy itself, and there, twinkling and calling brokenly for help, we sat on the sea and waited.

For a time it looked as though the navigation lights were coming no closer, and with a certain boyish glee Stanno began letting off the distress flares he'd found in a waterproof pouch. Then gradually the lights became larger and clearer, and above the noise of the light breeze we could hear the heavy beat of engines.

"I think it's the *Trebizond,* all right," said Selby. The farsighted Javits had provided us with a Polaroid snapshot of the ship before we left Ancona; with the deck lights full on to inspire us, we could recognize the configuration of the ship's superstructure. Then, as suddenly as they had come on, they were turned off again, and the ship seemed to vanish.

"So they can see us," I said, to forestall the inevitable question from Stanno. I suppose if you spend most of your time on foot patrols round the Ballymurphy Estate, you do become a bit of a landlubber. A searchlight flicked on from the bridge, and the beam flopped onto the waves about twenty yards away before veering over and bathing us in painful brilliance.

"Shit," remarked Selby. "What a nasty business being rescued is."

"Just try to look grateful like any other crashed airman," I said. The repeater bell of the ship's telegraph jingled out across the waves. The throb of the engines increased, and water churned at the stern as the engines began to kill the momentum.

"Can anyone see the name?" I asked the others.

"No," said Stanno. "I can't see a fucking thing with that light."

A loud-hailer clicked on with a metallic hiccup.

"We are coming alongside," a voice boomed out above the noise of the engines.

"What an arsehole," said Stanno.

"He might have been sending a boat," I told him reasonably. "It was wise of him to let us know."

Although the dinghy was not moving, we seemed to slide slowly in under the black cliff of hull that hung above us. The deck lights came on, including the hand-directed lamp at the head of the companionway that had been lowered. A rope fell into the water a yard away, and Selby made it fast to the dinghy. It had been a fine piece of seamanship not to overshoot a little rubber dot in the sea at night, and I was impressed.

"Okay," I said in a low voice, "remember we don't want the wireless operator to radio our false identities; otherwise we'll have the Americans out here in helicopters. We don't waste time, all right? And act it up a bit."

The ship's engines were now a pulse so deep that they scarcely interfered with the silence that now fell. In the shelter of the ship's side there was no wind, and a clear voice with a slight accent spoke English from somewhere over our heads.

"Ahoy there," it said. "Do any of you require immediate medical assistance?"

"No," I shouted back.

"Stand by and we'll help you aboard."

Two seamen came down the companionway and stood on the square grating that formed its lowest step. They helped

71

us out of the dinghy in turn and followed us as we slowly staggered upwards towards the interested faces that hung in a row over the rail. At the head of the stairs stood a spruce, dark-complexioned man of about forty in white trousers and with a cap tucked under one arm.

"Captain Ratnayaka," he said to each of us in turn, and he shook us each by the hand. "Welcome aboard the *Trebizond*. Are you well and healthy?"

I'd already noticed the name painted on a life belt half-way up the companionway and was feeling immoderately pleased that at least we had got the right ship.

"Lieutenant Kowalski, U.S. Air Force," I said. "We're all okay, thanks, Captain. Boy, are we glad to see you." I glimpsed the other two nodding vehemently. "It was getting goddam cold out there, I can tell you."

"How long were you there, please? Are there any more of you?"

"Oh, coupla hours at the most. We're the only ones."

"We can find hot food quickly. Also new clothes too, of course. But please you can give me first the name of where you are from and your aeroplane—you were in an aeroplane?—so that I can send messages to your air force that you are safe."

"No, Captain." It was Selby, who had edged round so as to be behind him and was now training that vast pistol on him. In the semi-darkness, the gun looked like a black pig's leg. Stanno and I got our backs to the rail simultaneously, Stanno producing his Sterling with commendable speed, slapping a thirty-four-round magazine into the side and pulling the cocking handle rearwards with practiced efficiency. Meanwhile, I struggled to produce the riot gun from under my flying suit, where I had held it beneath one arm as if incapacitated by an injury. There seemed to be an endless embarrassing wait as I disentangled the damn thing from the front zip.

"Nobody moves," I said, cradling the weapon at last, making my meaning clear for anybody who had neither English nor intelligence by sweeping the muzzle in a slow arc.

"I do not understand," said Captain Ratnayaka, standing very stiffly. "I have rescued you."

"Thanks, Captain," I said. "You did fine, and you still are. We don't want to hurt you or your crew, so just tell them to keep very quiet. I'll explain later. First, how many are there aboard?"

"Twenty-two, including myself."

I did a quick head count. It left six elsewhere in the ship.

"Selby, take that man nearest you and find the WO. Nobody else moves."

Selby indicated the sailor with a jerk of the Ruger. The seaman, a young lad of about eighteen, looked the color of paper in the loading lights.

"Does he understand English?" I called after Selby, and his charge nodded vigorously.

"This is piracy," said Captain Ratnayaka. "If he hurts my crewman, it will be murder too."

"He won't, Captain—not if the man does what he's told—and neither will . . ." I sensed movement over on my left where there should have been none, swung and fired. The weapon kicked viciously in my hands, and I was momentarily blinded by the muzzle flash. There was a thud on the planking, and I saw that half the upper portion of the man's body had been blown out over the Adriatic. The rail behind where he had been standing had been sprayed red for a stretch of several feet. In the singing silence that fell after the monstrous explosion, nothing moved except one of the man's feet, which twitched several times. As an object lesson, it was made twice as effective by the way the man had fallen, the open abdomen, chest and thoracic cavity uppermost, with a stump of neck protruding at the top. A clinching detail was his right hand, severed raggedly at the mid-forearm, still grasped firmly round the butt of what looked like a Smith & Wesson Centennial halfway out of his trouser pocket.

"I do not believe this," said Captain Ratnayaka. One of the seamen began vomiting over his own feet, making gestures with his hands to indicate that he was not moving of his own volition.

"All you have to believe, Captain, is that I mean what I say. Did you know that man was armed?"

"No. On my word, no."

"I think you'll find three more like him aboard," I said. "You might not have known this but they planned to hijack your ship."

"The ones who joined at Trieste."

I nodded. There came a call from up by the bridge.

"Lee? You all right down there?"

"Yup," I shouted. I recognized Selby's voice.

"I'm coming out with the kid and the wireless operator. Okay?"

"Fine."

He stepped out into the light a safe distance behind the two men, who glanced down onto the glinting red area of the floodlit deck and seemed to hesitate.

"Who was that you blasted?" called Selby.

"One of the opposition," I said. "Did you get the WO in time?"

"Uh-huh. He was standing by, waiting for the Captain to tell him what to send. The wireless room's now locked, and I've got the key."

"Good man. Right!" I shouted. "Now I want everybody lined up along the edge of number three hatches facing inboard; is that clear? You move very slowly, and you put both hands on top of your heads *now*. Okay, move." While Stanno, Selby and I watched with our backs to the rail, the men moved over to form a line along the edge of the hold, pressing the middle of their shins against the tarpaulin-layered hatch covers. "Now, when I say, 'Go,' you will kneel on the edge of the hatch and then fall forward onto your faces. Your hands will remain on top of your heads all the time—you will not break your fall with them; is that clear?"

Several of the seamen turned round with faces that were severally frightened, questioning or just plain angry.

"Captain," I said, "you had better translate into whatever language you need. I don't have to remind you of what will happen if it turns out to have been a bad translation."

"No," said Ratnayaka, "you do not." He spoke a few sentences in a language I didn't recognize and then followed up with some Spanish, which slightly surprised me. One doesn't necessarily expect a Panamanian ship to have any Spanish-speaking crew aboard.

"You frisk them," I said to Stanno and Selby; "I'll watch the bridge." I raised my voice. "Go," I shouted, and the line of men sank slowly to their knees before falling forward onto their faces. Some of them did nothing to break their fall; some tried to get one shoulder or the other onto the canvas-covered boards before their noses; others crouched forward and "walked" on their elbows until we had fifteen men in a row on their faces, their boot soles thrust towards us. Careful to avoid getting in my line of fire, Stanno and Selby frisked each one with meticulous thoroughness. It was a pleasure to watch Stanno, in particular. I'd wondered whether all those snap searches in Northern Ireland might not have made him overfamiliar with the procedure and therefore a bit careless. Quite the reverse: he knew all the places and missed nothing. Two pistols, both automatics, and five knives in all. They were a good team, he and Selby. It was people like that they needed on Security at London Airport.

"Don't forget number seventeen," I said when they had finished, but Stanno was already walking towards the body. He stooped down and plucked the stump of arm with its dead hand still clutching the gun out of the trouser pocket and tossed it over the side. Then he grasped the remaining arm and turned the body over to check the other pockets. That was nice: it was professional and made me feel confident; but it also made a mess because all the man's viscera fell out onto the deck with a noise like wet eels being poured from a bucket.

"What the hell are you shooting in that thing?" Stanno asked. "Howitzer shells?"

"Just number four shot at the moment," I said. "Ordinary Hi-Vel load." I scanned the bridge and deck in both directions, wondering where the missing five were. The ship lay almost motionless in the water, the deck trembling slightly as the engines ticked over, the soft roar of the exhausts coming from the funnel mouth. "Please get up, Captain," I called, and Ratnayaka got to his feet stiffly, as if he were still in shock. His cap lay where it had fallen when he had put his hands on his head. He caught sight of the dead seaman and looked away.

"That is a disgusting weapon to use," he said.

"No, it's not." I shook my head. "Weapons are made to kill, not to provide sporting chances. This isn't a film set, where people get neat little holes through their upper arms, Captain. If someone pulls a gun on me I try to get him first, and I don't aim to let him have a second chance."

"You pulled a gun on all of us," said Ratnayaka. He shook his head. "We stopped to rescue you. It is the code of the sea."

"I've already thanked you," I pointed out. "What you can't get into your head is that there were already men on board who were going to hijack your ship. We're trying to save you from them, if you like." I regretted not being able to explain the full irony at the moment, but the Captain anyway had quite a few more surprises in store for him. "If you don't believe me, you can watch this." I turned to address his crew, who still lay on the hatches. "When I say so, you will get up slowly and turn this way," I sang out. "Hands still on the head. Go!"

The men lined up against the edge of the hatch covers once more, watching us and trying to keep their eyes off what lay on the deck before them.

"This is the final chance for some of you," I said clearly. "I want all those employed by Mr. Brückner to step forward now. I should warn you that if you do not and I discover your association later, I personally will shoot you." I gestured with the High Standard and indicated the bloody rail. I turned to Selby. "You'd better repeat that in Italian," I said. He did so, and instantly two men stepped forward, their eyes round with fear.

77

"Ask how many more of them there are aboard," I told Selby.

"One," he said after a brief exchange. "He's in the engine-room. Shall I get him?"

"No," I said. "Stanno, escort Captain Ratnayaka to the bridge and have him get on the speaking tube to the engine-room and everywhere else belowdecks. I want the whole crew here, and that includes the man at the helm." The Captain looked at me sharply.

"Lieutenant Kowalski, it is an offense to leave the ship to drift with no persons manning her," he said. "There is great danger of collision."

"That's my risk, Captain," I said. "If you knew it, I'm doing you a favor. You ought to be glad to have someone to flush out the thugs who have infiltrated your crew."

He merely looked at me, and Stanno took him away. They soon reappeared, and one by one the remaining crew members started arriving from below. Three men came out of a hatchway towards the stern, and I swung my gun towards them.

"Halt!" I shouted.

"Identify your colleague," Selby told one of his two captives in Italian. The man raised a hand and indicated the one on the right, a heavily built young man who was probably no more than seventeen or eighteen. "Hands on head, step forward," commanded Selby—but the boy had now seen the corpse, which seemed to affect him more powerfully than the sight of the guns in our hands. Instead of trying to get back down the hatchway, which he might just have managed, he panicked and made a dash across the deck towards a stretch of the far rail that lay in comparative darkness. Personally, I wouldn't have fired, because he'd made no attempt to draw a weapon, but Stanno gave the boy a short burst, which caught him across the small of the back and the buttocks and slammed him into the rail. He could be heard crying in the scuppers for a few seconds before silence fell again. Stanno walked over, his Sterling at the ready in front of him, and stooped down in the shadows. Then he straightened up and came back, shaking his head at me. "Unarmed," he said. "Not even a knife." He sounded disgusted.

"Murderers," said Captain Ratnayaka.

"Was that kid one of the ones you signed on at Trieste?" I asked him.

"Yes."

"He might have wound up killing you. They were going to take the ship over at some point."

"That boy?" asked the Captain incredulously.

"That boy and his three mates," I agreed. "Plus reinforcements under a man named Brückner who is liable to arrive at any moment, I don't yet know how. Okay, I want to say a few words to your crew, Captain, and then we'll get this show back on the road. I'll give you a new course in just a moment."

With Selby interpreting, followed unwillingly by the Captain, I told the crew of the *Trebizond* that they had just been saved from being taken over by unscrupulous pirates. I added that there would be no more violence if it could possibly be avoided, and although I was sure that several of the crew had knives or guns down below, there would be no future in trying to use them—indeed, no point whatever, as the ship and her Captain were safe. I apologized for the inconvenience and had Ratnayaka dismiss them. There wasn't much chatter as they filed back to work, leaving behind two bodies and the two living members of the group who had joined at Trieste.

"Let's go back to the bridge, Captain," I suggested. "We'll take these two bandits with us and see if we can extract some information. Stan, would you get the extra ammo from the dinghy, then scuttle it. After that, find a deckhand to weight the bodies and get them over the side. I want you to see them go, okay?"

"Right." He slung his Sterling and vanished down the steps over the ship's side. Selby marched the two Italians on ahead, and the Captain and I brought up the rear. Once on the bridge, I told him to resume his original course and speed. When he had given the orders, the telegraph had rung up full speed ahead and the *Trebizond* was once again under way, I produced a letter from inside my flying suit and gave it to him.

"Read that," I said, "and set your mind at rest." It was an idea that had occurred to me at the last moment back in Ancona; there was no need to complete the entire voyage at gunpoint. Ratnayaka took the letter.

"You are working for Mr. Javits?" he inquired at length.

"Right," I said. "That's his signature at the bottom, as you know. He learned that there'd be an attempt to take over the ship, but the information only reached him after you'd sailed yesterday. Obviously he couldn't radio you, not knowing who was in the plot. I'm sure I can rely on you to follow the change-of-course instructions."

"Malta," said Ratnayaka.

"Malta," I agreed. "Don't worry, Mr. Javits will meet us there in person. Now, Captain, I know this is your bridge and you are in command here, but I would be grateful if you'd let me interrogate these two; I want to know what to expect." I waved a hand at the heavies—who were glowering, but not so much that they couldn't switch the expression to one of placation if necessary.

"Very well," he said in a resigned voice. They don't build these nautical types the way they used to. They're all soul nowadays. It's that delicate balance between the lash, sodomy and rum that has disappeared; you can run anything with a combination of discipline, affection and insensibility. It's fatal to concentrate on any one of them, but I suppose this is the age of specialization. I wondered vaguely where Captain Ratnayaka stood. He didn't look like a drunkard.

Selby clicked back the hammer of his Ruger and raised the gun, firing off a question in Italian as he did so. The men flinched, and both began talking simultaneously. After a time, Selby made a motion with the muzzle of his pistol, and they fell silent again.

"Dawn tomorrow," he said. "We've got thirty hours. They think it'll be either the disabled-fishing-boat gag or the stoker with acute peritonitis."

"How many?"

"They don't know. Probably another four, and they expect Brückner as well."

I turned to Ratnayaka. "Satisfied, Captain?" I asked.

"I suppose I must be, Lieutenant," he said.

"You can drop the 'Kowalski' bit, Captain. Plain 'Mr. Lee' will do. I have no more connection with the USAF than you have. Now"—I moved over to a chart of the Adriatic—"where will we be thirty hours from now?"

Captain Ratnayaka frowned. "We're making about twenty knots. Here, I should think," and he placed a brown forefinger in the sea off the toe of Italy.

"Right. It looks as though they'll come from Reggio," I told Selby.

"What do we do?" he asked. I shrugged.

"Lock these two up, get some food and sleep," I said. "And wait. What else?"

10

For the remainder of that night and the rest of the following day, the *Trebizond* plowed steadily down the coast of Italy. Her decks had been hosed down, and from all appearances the ship had returned to normal. Even Captain Ratnayaka seemed to have got over the ruffling his nautical propriety had suffered. Stanno, Selby and I took turns in patrolling the ship, but we neither expected nor experienced trouble.

Selby woke me at four o'clock the following morning.

"Any sign of Brückner?" I asked as he handed me a cup of tea without milk in it. Some Indian in the galley, probably.

"Nothing except lights coming up on the starboard bow," he said. "Ratnayaka thinks they're fishing boats."

"It's a pity we don't know exactly where he hopes to board the ship," I said, sipping. Tannin furred the roof of my mouth. "Thing is, the Captain's going to have to alter course soon. As long as we've been in the Adriatic, it hasn't mattered whether we were heading for Tripoli or the Straits of Gibraltar. But he can't leave it later than Reggio."

"You sound as if you're anxious to meet Brückner," said Selby. "Despite his reputation."

"I'm not," I confessed. "I'd much rather hug the Greek coast all the way down to Pilos and then go southwest across the Med. That way he'd never find us. But we *want* him to find us."

"Quite," agreed Selby. "Otherwise he alerts Anscudden that somebody's got there first. Do we shoot it out?"

"We'll have to play it by ear. If we can take them all and just lock them up until we get to Malta, then that would be fine. What we must do is prevent anyone from getting away."

I had finished breakfast and was watching the gray dawn through the clear-view panels on the bridge. I had borrowed a pair of Captain Ratnayaka's binoculars and regularly covered the ever-increasing horizon in slow sweeps. Cape Spartivento was coming up to starboard—a low chunk of land that was the extreme point of the Italian peninsula.

"Not a thing," I said, and I handed the glasses to Selby. Stanno had cleaned his Sterling and was now checking the staggered loading of rounds in his spare magazines. The numb unreality that seems to be inseparable from dawn was giving way to a tension which afflicted no one so much as Captain Ratnayaka. He paced the bridge ceaselessly, peering in turn at the binnacle, at the engineroom repeater and out of the window. He even scrutinized a couple of ammeters every few minutes, though God knows what good it did him.

"I do not like this, Mr. Lee," he said. "I do not like this at all. I am not the commander of a warship, you know. I am the skipper of a merchantman who is taking a load of clay to Dar-es-Salaam. Mr. Javits has chartered this vessel, and it is costing him sixteen hundred dollars a day, so I am bound to go where he tells me. But I do not like it, this stupid fighting and bloodshed."

It was Selby who spotted it first; a white cabin cruiser rolling in the long swell two miles away. A distress flare arched up against the gray morning overcast.

"That's original," he said.

Captain Ratnayaka prepared to heave the *Trebizond* to once more.

"Remember to play it as planned, Captain," I said, "and it should be fairly painless. We'll stay under cover until they're all aboard. Good luck." I tucked the High Standard under my arm. This time I was loading the heavy sabot rounds only.

"If it's any consolation to you, Captain," said Selby in his most gentlemanly manner, "I think you're a damn fine seaman. You handle a ten-thousand-ton freighter as if it were a launch. I admire that, because it makes you a professional. We'll also try to be professional," he added in what he probably hoped was a reassuring tone—but it might well have sounded chilling to the Captain, whose mouth set in a narrow line as he went about bringing the ship to a stop.

We dispersed to the various positions we'd previously decided upon. I crouched outside a wing of the bridge overlooking the steps up which Brückner would come from the launch. Stanno stood inside a tarpaulin draped over the winch assembly of the No. 3 hold loading crane. Selby was hidden down towards the stern near the after companionway that led to the engineroom. From my position, I had a perfect view of the maneuvering that brought the *Trebizond* alongside the white launch as gently as it had nudged up to our rubber dinghy some thirty hours before.

85

Selby had been right: Captain Ratnayaka's seamanship was impeccable. I heard the engineroom-telegraph bell signal Stop, and the Captain stepped out a moment later. On his way down he had to pass me, so I stuck up my thumb in a friendly gesture of congratulation, but he chose to ignore me.

I watched as, twenty or so feet below me, the scene of our own boarding was replayed. Brückner was the first one up: a tall blond man of about my age who, although thin, moved with a gracefulness that betrays fine muscular co-ordination. I had seen him once before in Hamburg and had thought then that I didn't much want to go up against him. Now, at closer range, I was damn sure I didn't. Behind him came three more men, two of whom were clearly from the same mold as the Trieste mob. The other had something of Brückner's look about him, although he was a physically different type, being extremely broad.

"It was good of you to stop, Captain," said Brückner after they had introduced themselves. "We are in need of help." In his dark blue polo-necked sweater, he looked the soul of competence. As he spoke, his eyes were searching the deck and the superstructure. I gave a wan smile to see his three henchmen line up with their backs to the rail exactly as we had. When I saw Brückner produce his gun, I clicked on the microphone I had hitched by an extension cord to the ship's loud-hailer.

"Hold it right there, Brückner," I said. "You're all covered. Drop your weapons and you'll live. Now!" I barked. The sound blatted metallically among the iron ladders and gangways.

Christ, the man was fast. He'd involuntarily looked up-wards towards the source of the sound, but had realized almost instantly that it was irrelevant for locating the person speaking. Then, before anybody else could move, Brückner had darted forward into the doorway that led to the *Trebizond*'s saloon, past a frozen crew member, who effectively blocked him from the view of both Stanno and Selby. As the door was immediately beneath me, I also lost sight of him.

Not much slower to react had been Brückner's thickset colleague, who sprang sideways and got an arm round Ratnayaka's neck from behind. One of the other two men was not so bright. He automatically jerked up his pistol and blazed away in my direction. A bullet ricocheted off the side of the bridge about ten feet from me; another struck a wire stay with a sound like a giant banjo being plucked. Crouched behind my corner of coaming, I was in little danger, but thought it was time Stanno took a hand.

At that moment, the Sterling opened up from below. It was copybook shooting: two short bursts which hit each man in turn at chest height. I could see the tiny spurts of dust and fabric particles as the bullets tore through their clothing. But even as Stanno was firing, the broad man had begun to back rapidly away forward, still holding Captain Ratnayaka in front of him like a shield. The Captain's face looked darker than usual and, because his captor was a head shorter, he was being bent over backwards. I crawled rapidly along behind the coaming so as to keep them in sight, trailing microphone cable. Unfortunately for the heavy, there was not much cover for some yards. He would have noticed and rejected the lifeboat on its davits to his left as being too flimsy and too far off the deck to prevent his feet from being seen. He chose the forward companion-way, reaching back with his gun hand to pull open the

87

hatch, which I had foresightedly dogged only half an hour earlier.

I briefly checked that I had a sabot round chambered, brought the High Standard up on aim with my right hand and with my left thumbed the mike switch.

"Okay, Stan, I'll take him," I said, and the noise of the loudspeaker was enough to distract the man for an instant. He must have thought he was being covered from behind, for he jerked his head back to see. At that moment he gave me a target, and I fired. Many things happened at once. The light weapon, never intended for one-handed firing, kicked viciously, and the side of the receiver caught me a terrific blow on my cheek which brought little sparks shooting across the retina of my right eye. Simultaneously, I saw Captain Ratnayaka's head turn into a red ball before he and the man collapsed onto the deck planking. As a feeling of bitter disappointment came over me, I was suddenly aware of a new noise. An engine note rose to a howl, and it took a moment in my dazed state before I had identified it. Then I saw the white launch surge away from under the *Trebizond*'s forefoot in a steep canting swath of foam, twin exhausts lacing the wash with gray smoke.

"Shit!" my voice boomed out over the ship, startling me. I had forgotten that I was still clutching the mike.

Selby was firing carefully over the rail in the classic two-handed stance of a professional, the barrel of the Blackhawk Special steadied on the varnished wood. I saw him get off all six, but only observed one visible impact, when a corner of the cabin roof exploded in a cloud of splinters. By now the launch was eighty yards away and seemed to be mechanically quite undamaged. Blessing the impulse that had made me fill the tube magazine of the riot gun with sabot rounds rather than shot, I steadied the gun on a handy brass rail and took careful aim.

If you're a right-handed shot like me, the proper firing stance for the High Standard Model 10 when you are resting it on a solid support is for the left hand to come across the body and hold the butt plate into your right shoulder. There's no stock—just this curved and swiveling piece of metal at the end of the weapon, which fits the contour of the shoulder quite nicely. The only thing is that your trigger hand is holding the gun by a pistol grip halfway along its length, which means that when the weapon's fired, the recoil tends to throw up the muzzle and push down the butt plate, making it pivot around your right wrist. When I'd fired it single-handed, exactly this had happened, and the side of my face felt huge and glossy. Now I was more cautious, clamping the plate into my shoulder and getting the launch into my open sights.

It was one of those medium-sized motorboats that have everything enclosed except for a small well at the rear of the cabin. I couldn't see the man at the wheel and had no idea even which side the wheel was on. Still, I tried one shot to the left of the cabin door and another to the right. I saw the second sabot strike because it hit a small red fire extinguisher clipped outside, producing a white explosion of foam. The craft veered violently to the left and set off on a new tack, its speed undiminished. I now had a larger target area to choose from and tried a shot about a foot above the waterline and where I hoped the engine would be. The result was immediate and impressive. The powerful roar died as if a recording had been switched off, and the launch lost way, the bows sinking back into the sea.

But I couldn't leave it there: the craft still had a radio,

and while I thought there was probably only one man aboard, who would not have had time to get a message off, it was conceivable that there might be somebody with him who would have the presence of mind to ignore the bullets and put out a call. Either way, the continued existence of the antenna rig on top of the cabin was a hazard. Luckily, there was a good solid object in the center of all those thin whip aerials: the sabot struck the base of the miniature coastal radar dish and wiped the whole installation into the sea thirty feet away, leaving a ragged hole in the roof where it had been torn out by the roots. Silence fell.

That left Brückner at liberty somewhere on the ship. I stood up and touched my right cheek gingerly with my fingertip. It felt in flames; but no bones broken, no spongy depressions. I kicked an ejected case out of the way and picked up the microphone.

"Everyone will stay just where they are until we find the last man," I said, and I clapped a hand over the mike with a bang as the echoes began to build up a howl of feedback. Then I took my hand away and added, "Selby, stay where you are, please. Stan, come with me," clicked off the switch and went down the companionway to the main deck. There was a commotion up towards the bows, and I saw Captain Ratnayaka being lifted up. His head and shoulders were a crimson sheen of blood, spattered with pink and white blobs. To my considerable surprise, he pushed away the supporting hands and stood up by himself, slowly massaging his throat.

He looked up and took a few unsteady steps towards me. "You shoot well, sir," he said painfully, and he winced.

"Where are you hurt?" I inquired. The Captain pointed at his throat.

"That man, he had arms like hawsers." He looked towards where his attacker lay.

His ex-captor seemed to be all in one piece except that his head was missing, and even that was around. All around, I saw, noticing the spray of brain tissue and bone chips that covered everything in the vicinity. At that moment, Captain Ratnayaka seemed to realize what it was that kept sliding stickily down his face. His hand went to his cheek, and he examined the blob with horror. With a great effort of self-control, he compressed his lips and held himself very straight. When the spasm of nausea had passed, he opened his eyes, ran his tongue round his mouth and spat.

"Wash," was all he said.

"Later," I said shortly. "One of them's still on the loose. You stay where you are."

I retrieved the man's gun from where it had fallen. A Browning Hi-Power automatic, I saw, with a checkered walnut stock. Takes the 9mm Parabellum, thirteen shots before you have to reload. A nice handgun—reliable, and pretty accurate in the hands of a marksman because the rear sight's adjustable for windage. I slipped it into my pocket.

Stanno came up, snapping a fresh magazine into the Sterling.

"How do we get Brückner?" he asked.

"I don't know," I admitted. "The only thing he can hope to do is get to the radio room and try to send a message."

"Good job Selby locked it," said Stanno. We turned to look up at the port side of the bridge just in time to see the thin figure of Brückner reach the top of the stairway that led to the WO's quarters. Stanno got off a short, deafening burst of fire, but he was shooting from the waist, and the bullets merely knocked off some paint and broke a small porthole. Then we were running towards the stairs, knowing he could shoot off the lock of the wireless room but also knowing that he would not have time to send a message. We reached the stairs. Still no sound from above.

"He'll go down," I said to Stanno. "He'll try and buy himself some time." He nodded, and we made for the door that led down to the galley. If we were quick enough, I reckoned we could capitalize on having outthought Brückner by meeting him on his way down from the bridge. We clattered down the iron stairway.

Down there it was quiet and warm. We stood, trying not to pant, listening for a sudden rush of steps down the forward companionway that led out of the administrative regions of varnished wood and into the functional areas of painted metal where we were. We could see the foot of the stairs about twenty feet away, separated from us by a passageway, lined with handrails, off which led the quarters of the cook and other crew members. Still not a footstep.

Then, from far away behind us, there came the flat sound of a gunshot.

"Jesus," said Stanno. "How did the bugger get there?"

We turned and raced down one of the passages that led down the side of the hull, past portholes with their covers latched up through which gray light filtered, until we reached a bulkhead with a steep ladder leading downwards. A hot draft of oily air met us, together with the clattering throb of idling diesel engines. We went down the steps fast and found ourselves high up in the engineroom. In the middle lay a huge well of air, a sheer thirty-foot drop down to the green-painted valve covers of the twin motors, past which emerged two thickly lagged exhaust flues joining near our heads to form a great tube three feet in diameter which disappeared upwards towards the funnel. Round this gulf ran gridded metal catwalks in layers which corresponded to the ship's decks. On the catwalk below us and opposite a man lay outstretched, a long heavy screwdriver in one hand and a ball of oily rag in the other. He was on his back, and the front of his overalls was bright with blood. Automatically, we ran to the nearest steps leading down to the lower level before I worked out that it was what we were expected to do. I glanced up to the corner diagonally opposite, and there was the pale gleam of Brückner's blond hair as he waited for a clear shot. I swerved to knock Stanno sideways behind a thick cluster of pipes. A bullet splashed off the catwalk six inches from my foot and hit something the other side of the engine room with a dull clang. As if we had rehearsed the move together, Stanno dropped to the metal floor and stuck out his head and the Sterling at the base of the pipework, getting off a burst of fire to cover me. The ruse worked, for Brückner's shot went high—where Stanno's head would have been if he had emerged at normal height. That was the signal for me to spring out and let rip with the riot gun.

At that moment, I bitterly regretted not having a normal cartridge of heavy shot. Even with all that metalwork in the way, something would get through, whereas a single projectile stood little chance of going straight between the inch-wide interstices of the catwalk. No time to aim properly, either. I thought as I squeezed the trigger that Brückner had managed to get another shot off, but its sound was drowned in the roar of the High Standard. The effect of my own shot was dramatic, however. I had forgotten how brittle cast iron is. The heavy bullet must have struck the catwalk near Brückner's feet, for the whole of the immediate area seemed to shatter. The shock of the concentrated release of energy must have been enormous, for I could see his whole body jump into the air. He was thrown heavily against the guardrail, but unfortunately for him, he was at the end of a section, and the base of the final stanchion had been blasted completely away. He flung out a hand to steady himself, but missed by half an inch, sailing outwards and downwards in a shower of iron fragments to glance off one of the big motors three decks below.

Cautiously, men in overalls started emerging from behind whatever cover they had been able to find. Stanno was picking himself up, spots of blood down one side of his face.

"Hit?" I asked.

"Ricochet," he said, feeling the place and smearing it messily. He looked at his fingertips. "His second shot, I guess. It knocked sparks off the floor right next to me. He wasn't bad, was he?"

We walked quickly down the iron ladders until we reached the lowest level. Brückner was lying in a twisted heap half against the crankcase of the port engine. There was blood on both trouser legs, and he seemed to have soiled himself, and only then I remembered exactly why it was that we needed him alive.

"Shit," I said softly, and I picked up his gun from where it had slid nearby. Also a Browning Hi-Power, I noticed, identical to the one his broad colleague had been carrying. Then I noticed that Brückner's eyes were open and following my movements. I raised my gun automatically before lowering it again, feeling foolish.

"No need," said Brückner with difficulty, swallowing. "I can't move."

"Where are you hit?" I asked him, squatting down.

"I can't feel my legs. I think my back is broken." It would explain the relaxed sphincter muscles.

"I'm sorry about that," I said, and in a way I was. After all, Brückner meant nothing to me; he was just a man hired to do a job which conflicted with mine. Purely a matter of circumstances; at another time we might have found ourselves on the same side. "It's the job."

"Yes."

"How much was Anscudden paying you?" I asked. He rolled his head and tried a smile.

"Only ten grand. Half later."

"What was your next move going to be?"

Brückner managed the smile this time. He looked as genuinely amused as it is possible for a mortally injured man to look.

"Call him up. Ship-to-shore radio message. Tell him we'd pulled it off." He shook his head wryly.

"What were you to say?" I prompted. "Where is he?"

Brückner shut his eyes, and for a moment I thought he had died on me just when it was getting interesting. Then he opened them again tiredly.

"Shit, why should I care about Anscudden?" he asked. "There's not much he can do to me now. Not much anybody can, come to that."

"I promise you I'll get you evacuated by chopper just as soon as we can call up a rescue," I said.

"Waste of time. I was to have sent a cable to him, care of the British Consulate in Palermo."

From overhead somewhere came an anguished shout, but I ignored it and bent closer to Brückner, who moistened his lips.

"Code, I suppose." He spelled out three words. "Whatever they may mean. I told him why couldn't he give me something simple, and he said they were an old favorite of his."

"What a classy bastard." I felt a cold fury at something that was so typically Anscudden. There was the sound of running feet behind. I stood up and turned. It was an engineer in stained overalls, his hands sticky with blood and his face staring with anger. Before I could move, he had given a great shout and barged me aside. Then he was kicking at Brückner's head repeatedly, his right shoe smashing into the face and neck, panting with emotion. Stanno got his arms round him from behind, but was violently heaved away. It took several of the other engineers who had been gathering round to subdue him, but by that time it was too late.

"What the hell did you do that for?" I shouted at the struggling man. He began a high-pitched explanation in yet another language I didn't understand.

"That man," explained a fellow in a singlet, pointing a finger at Brückner's battered head, "he kill his friend"—and he indicated his heaving colleague before jerking the finger upwards. I remembered the body we had seen on the way down.

"I see," I said.

Stanno and I left them to it and walked back up to find Selby. As we emerged on deck, the early-morning breeze struck fresh and cool, and I became aware of how hot it had been in the engineroom. Selby had his gun on us as we came through the door and then relaxed.

"You got him?" he asked. "I heard the shooting." I nodded.

"We knocked him down and one of the crew finished him off. Look, we've got a cable to send to Anscudden. He and Brückner had an arrangement so that he could be told that the snatch had been successful."

"I'll get the WO and unlock the door," said Selby, tucking the Ruger into the waistband of his trousers. "Where do we send it and what's the message?"

"Cable to Anscudden, care of British Consulate Palermo. The message is . . . er . . . Jesus, I think I've forgotten it. It's in a foreign language."

"That's helpful. You mean it's nothing to do with the arms?"

"Got it," I said. "It's *'Furor arma ministrat.'* "

"Fancy that," said Selby. "Sounds like Latin or something. Here, you'd better come and spell it out for me. One thing about a message like that: nobody would ever hit on it by chance."

Which I suppose was why I admired Selby so much. I'll bet he'd done bloody Latin at school—all officers and gentlemen have. And I'll bet he even knew what it meant, too.

When we had sent this cryptic sentence, we came back and found Stanno going through the pockets of the men he had killed on deck: a total of four hundred and fifty dollars, a knife and two cheap Spanish handguns. Meanwhile, Selby set about arranging for the launching of a dinghy, and a few minutes later its bulky bottom smacked the sea.

"There's no need for you to come," I told Selby. "Stan and I can handle that motorboat." I jerked a thumb to where the shot-up launch lay rocking gently a hundred yards from the ship. "Why not get some of the crew to weight the bodies and get rid of them? Then you might find out how that poor sod Ratnayaka is: it's been a rough couple of days for him, and he's still got to get this tub to Malta. Tell him to go and have a bath; that'll cheer him up." He nodded and strode off.

"Excitable buggers, aren't they?" said Stanno as we climbed into the dinghy. "Kicking each other to death. I'll cover you if you want to row."

"I don't," I said shortly.

"Well, I don't know how to row, do I?" He scrambled forward and sat up in the bows, smacking another magazine into the Sterling before cocking the gun. He was going to have to do a lot of magazine recharging after this was over, I could see. "Do you reckon on any oppo, Lee?" he called.

"No idea," I said, taking the oars and pulling unskillfully away from the *Trebizond*. "I couldn't see anybody all the time I was shooting. Could be that some bastard has us in his sights right now."

"Uh-huh. If we go bows on to her, there'll be less to hit. Right hand down a bit . . . no, sorry, I mean left."

We plowed an erratic course across the intervening hundred or so yards of water. I kept turning my head to see where we were heading and noticed that the launch—which I could now see was called *La Canicola*—had taken on a slight list to port as it lay in the water. I also thought it had settled a bit, so perhaps it was holed somewhere. After a bit, I stopped rowing and we drifted in alongside. Nothing moved, and there was no sound other than the gurgle and slap of the waves. Stanno sprang up on the launch's deck, his Sterling at the ready, searching the blind windows for signs of life.

"Outside slowly with your hands empty," he shouted. There was no reply. His voice fell flat in the early-morning air. I hitched the dinghy's painter to a stanchion and joined him on *La Canicola*'s deck. We split up and each sidled down the narrow gangway between the wall of the cabin and the rail, moving down towards the stern, where Stanno jumped down into the well and burst into the cabin. The whole afterpart of the boat was covered in foam from the holed extinguisher, I noticed, and my feet slipped on it as I followed Stanno in.

There was one person inside, and he was dead. He was leaning forward in the high-backed chair behind the wheel, his face resting among the dials and switches of the instrument panel.

"That sure is a gun you've got there," said Stanno, his right thumb automatically clicking the Sterling's change lever back to Safe.

The shot that had struck to the right of the cabin door had gone clear through the fire extinguisher and the cabin wall before hitting the padded oval metal back support of the helmsman's chair. It had blasted through this, taking with it a fist-sized wad of upholstery which it had carried through the man's body beyond. The bullet had gone on through the instrument panel and, for all I knew, right out at the bows and was still traveling. The man looked Italian —a middle-aged, grizzled individual with *Nina* tattooed on one forearm. Above his head was a gaping hole where the radio aerials had been.

"You should see the mess in here," Stanno's voice came from behind. He had lifted up the engine-compartment hatch in the floor and was on his knees looking down. The first thing I noticed was a strong smell of petrol. The light glinted on a black surging.

"Looks like water's getting in fast," I said. The list had

indeed become more pronounced. "At least one tank's holed, and I think that carburetor assembly is smashed. Boy, do those slugs have some power! Okay, let's move out."

"What about the boat?" asked Stanno. "Do we just leave it here?"

I thought for a minute. "No," I said, "we've got to get rid of it. That way there'll be no trace at all of Brückner's lot. Let's move out. We should be able to finish it off with all that petrol swilling about."

We went back outside, and I noted how badly damaged the superstructure was. Selby's great magnum rounds had smashed large holes in several places, and one of them had probably accounted for damage that was now below the waterline. We climbed into the dinghy and cast off.

"Better leave it till we get back," Stanno urged me. "There's probably quite a lot of fuel on board."

"I was going to."

We reached the *Trebizond*, and while a couple of crew members set about winching the dinghy back inboard, I drew a careful bead on the launch with the High Standard. It took two shots. As the second slug struck, there was a dull thump from inside the craft; the cabin roof blew apart, and orange flames blossomed from the hull. I had expected a larger explosion, so perhaps one of the main tanks was unholed and already beneath the waves. In a couple of minutes all that was left of *La Canicola* was a raft of fire burning down to the waterline; then that too vanished with an audible hiss leaving nothing but a column of dark smoke and a rapidly dispersing wisp of steam in the morning air. It was a calm, gray Sunday morning and over on the distant headland all manner of bells would be tinkling and bonging, just as they would right up through Italy and across Europe: a huge cacophony of clappers and bronze, mercifully inaudible here in the Mediterranean. Just the brief clang of the engineroom telegraph as the *Trebizond* once more got under way on her interrupted journey.

11

Valletta was a hundred and sixty miles away, and we made it by six that night. We were on the bridge with a recovered but shaken Captain Ratnayaka. Lights were twinkling along the high castellated walls as the *Trebizond* rounded St. Elmo Point and moved slowly, if not majestically, into Grand Harbour.

"French Creek," he said hoarsely. I thought his neck was dark with bruises, but maybe it was the blackout on the bridge.

"That's what he said," I agreed. "According to the letter, it's the fourth inlet on the left."

Captain Ratnayaka sniffed. There were probably more nautical ways of giving instructions to a ship's master, but I couldn't see a lot wrong with this one. Finally we berthed alongside a wharf with Corradino Heights rising up to our right. A huge warehouse stretched the length of the ship; on its side was the name z. GRECH in white capitals. That conveyed nothing to me: half the people on Malta are called Grech.

Javits came up with the customs and immigration men.

"Hi," he said. "No problems?"

"None," I shook my head.

"It was appalling," said Captain Ratnayaka. He rang down Stop Both and turned away. The shudder under the planks died.

"Midnight," said Javits, showing his perfect teeth in a grin. "That's when you sail again, Captain. Before then we have a complete cargo swap."

"Two thousand tons?" asked Ratnayaka incredulously. "Not possible, Captain. I have three holds, two cranes to each hold and a maximum of ten tons safe working load on each crane. That means . . . " He shook his head. "A full load per crane every six minutes. It can't be done."

"Don't panic," said Javits. "There's a heavy tracked crane on the wharf, and I've got an army of dockers. It's got to be done and it's going to be done, so we may as well get on with it."

"My men are exhausted with worry, Mr. Javits."

"Okay, there's a bonus for everybody. Now will you hurry it up, please?"

"He's taken a bit of a bashing," I said as Captain Ratnayaka walked from the bridge with silent dignity.

"You look a bit swollen up too."

I touched my cheek. "Recoil," I said ruefully. "We had to do some shooting. Ratnayaka didn't go for it much."

"So okay. We give him the loot you got off the opposition. How much is it?"

"Six guns, five knives and a little upwards of six-fifty bucks."

"We keep the hardware. He gets the rest."

"Shit," said Stanno. "He'll be able to retire."

"He'll deserve to," I said.

It was a little after midnight before the last hatches were

back in place and the *Trebizond's* deck crews were roping down the tarpaulin covers. The intervening hours had been frantic with activity, and although I wasn't surprised that Javits and Ratnayaka should make an efficient team, I was amazed at the speed with which the cargo switch proceeded. As soon as the crates allegedly containing china clay and school lab equipment touched the quay, the pallets were scooped up by a fleet of forklift trucks, which took them straight into the warehouse. Inside, the design was such that there was a building within a building. In the high space perhaps thirty feet wide that ran all round the inner structure were neat mountains of crates: some the raw wood coffins with rope handles traditionally used for packing rifles; others more anonymous boxes with polyglot stencils on the outside. MEIERHOF SPIELZEUGE KÖLN, said one. KÍKOBA RIO IND. BRAS. read another. What Javits had to do with German toy manufacturers and Brazilian sportswear companies I could not guess.

The Czech consignment was packed into empty bays in piles ten feet high: two thousand tons of ammunition and eight tons of assault rifles. From the other side of the doorway were taken pallet loads of crates marked ISRAELECTRIX DOMESTIC IRONS TEL-AVIV. These were the ex-Libyan Lee-Enfields which were going back to Tripoli. Javits might have looked unfunny, but he had a mean sense of humor. When he could see that the loading was going as fast as it could, he unlocked a steel door and showed Selby, Stanno and myself into the inner building.

"Time for a Scotch," he said.

Although I've seen many a warehouse full of arms, I still get a thrill from that smell of gun oil and old Cosmoline and the view when the lights go on of racked weapons in tall rows with long, narrow passageways between them. It's like being in one of those libraries that have shelves of books like cliffs so high that you have to get a stepladder to read the titles. Only I can look up there and say "1909 Argentine Mauser" or "1903 Springfield" or "Madsen Light Automatic Rifle," running my hand along the array of stocks. I can plunge my hand into an open case of ammunition and say, "Forty-five ACP" or "Cal-fifty Browning tracer" or "Seven-point-five Schmidt Rubin."

"Christ, how many of these places have you got?" asked Stanno.

"Several," said Javits with easy evasiveness, pouring out four tumblers of Scotch. "One here, one there. It mounts up. You haven't been in a place like this before?"

"Only in the Army," said Stanno.

"Ah." Javits waved a hand. "We're anybody's army here—anybody's at all. It's just a question of money."

"You mean you've no government strings attached?"

"If by that you mean pressures, no. Not at present, anyway. I can be friendly with a government one day and in its bad books the next." The perfect teeth appeared again, but the pink eyes stayed motionlessly fixed on Stanno. "You sure ask a lot of questions, son."

"Sorry, sir; no offense." It was the first time I'd seen old Stan back down.

"He's only just out of the Army, Mr. Javits," I said. The pink eyes turned on me.

"I know he is, Lee, I know he is. Like he told me himself back in Italy." He looked at Stanno. "How was it, son? An honorable discharge or kinda AWOL?"

"Kind of," agreed Stanno.

"For the money?"

105

"Yeah. Mostly."

"Well, then, son, I'm sorry if I sounded heavy. Fact is, a bit of honest interest never did anyone much harm. It's when it kinda slops over into curiosity that you've got to watch it. So seeing you asked, I'll tell you. I'm an arms dealer; I make my living by supplying arms to anyone who pays. Now, there are whole lots of different kinds of people who do that. Some of them work for a particular government, selling that country's armaments. They're little more than vacuum-cleaner salesmen, if you ask me. Others are brokers who practically never touch a weapon. They get an order to fill and they lift a phone and call someone in Zürich who can lay his hands on, say, ten thousand nine-mil automatic pistols, and they make a deal.

"Then there are the guys they call munitions manipulators. They come in when there's a legitimate call out by a government department which they dare not let appear as an official order. For example"—Javits took a gulp of Scotch —"suppose a country in Latin America had a right-wing military regime which the U.S. Government felt obliged to denounce in public. You know, all that horseshit about freedom of speech, democracy, personal liberty, habeas corpus, police brutality, the whole bleeding-hearts bit. And supposing meanwhile the CIA agents on the ground in that country wanted to arm a bunch of guerrillas in order to provoke an uprising in a border area so as to threaten a neighboring government. That's not hypothetical, by the way," he added. "It happened a couple of years back.

"Well, in that case the CIA might go to one of these munitions manipulator guys and buy what they needed without acting as representatives of the White House. You follow me?" Stanno nodded. "On the other hand, the CIA might do it their own way." Now I saw Selby nod slightly, and I smiled. Javits caught my eye. "Can't think why I'm telling you all this crap when you could ask old Lee, here." A white thumb jerked in my direction. "He's been out in the Far East; he knows what I mean. So does Mr. Selby, here, I'll bet."

"I've got an inkling," said Selby.

"Right. I remember, for instance, the problems we had once in getting weapons to anti-Communist guerrillas up in Laos. The Geneva Accords said the areas were Pathet Lao–controlled and we had no business there, but the Agency reckoned that Uncle Sam had friends somewhere in among 'em who needed something to shoot with. There wasn't time to go pissin' around so we had some guys in Vietnam lift a few thousand M-16s out of U.S. Army stores and fly 'em in on the usual rice-and-bandages drop that Air America was doing under the USAID refugee program."

"Not strickly legit," I said.

"Not strictly," Javits agreed. "Which brings us down to about the last type of arms dealer—the gunrunner who doesn't care whether it's legal or not. He'll supply anyone anywhere. For a price."

"Where does that leave your own Corporation, Mr. Javits?" asked Stanno. He seemed to have regained his usual temerity. Javits set his tumbler down with a bang that echoed up and down the narrow corridors between the stacked weapons. From outside the iron door came the steady industrious sounds of shouting and forklift trucks being maneuvered.

"Us? Well, now, we're a little bit of all of them rolled into one, wouldn't you say, Lee? But first and last, son, I'm a private individual. No government or agency tells me what to do—not ever. I'm maybe not so big as Cummings, but I can be approached without everyone from Brussels to Beirut finding out within half an hour. That's more than old Sam can do. I maybe haven't got the largest stocks of hardware in the business, either, but we're not doing badly, are we, Lee? Well, gentlemen"—Javits stood up—"as from tonight I sure as hell have a lot of Czech Model fifty-eights."

"What's happening to them?" I asked.

"Your friend Mr. Selby, here, told me he could fix it up," said Javits, turning his pinkish gaze on me. "And I must say he's made a mean job of it. You may have noticed out there that moored behind the *Trebizond*'s a beat-up old freighter called the *Marmara*." He waved a hand in the direction of the quay. "As soon as the *Trebizond*'s left, we load the toys on the *Marmara,* and Ratnayaka takes them straight on to Dar-es-Salaam, as arranged. Sure, it cost a bit to fix, but the Tanzanians are paying well for delivery. Hell, the *Marmara* even belongs to the same goddam shipping company. No problem."

"Actually, it wasn't a complete snip," said Selby. "Old Ratnayaka objected, and he took a lot of squaring." I remembered that Selby had disappeared quite early in the unloading, and I had assumed that he was laying plans. "I had to induce the captains to swap ships, because to make sure the *Trebizond* gets safely out of the Med, we need this Libyan diversion to work and buy us time. For his own safety, Captain Ratnayaka couldn't have arrived in Tripoli with a lot of old Lee-Enfields when the Libyans knew he had left Trieste with a lot of new assault rifles. They'd take him apart to find out what had happened on the way. So I got hold of the *Marmara*'s captain, who turns out to be a Turk named

Demirel, and told him I was now paying him to take a small cargo to Tripoli in the *Trebizond*. Demirel's a fat, plausible guy who wears shades twenty-four hours a day. He liked the money, and he was quite happy to leave the *Marmara*. Oh, yes—and I also told him my name was Anscudden." Selby smiled. "I think that was rather neat."

"Yup," I said. "He's going to be a sensation in Tripoli."

"Isn't he? The Libyans won't be able to sharpen their hatchets fast enough."

Stanno looked around at us, his curly hair dusty under the high warehouse lights. "You've got it all worked out, you lot, haven't you?" he said, possibly with admiration.

"Just organization, son," said Javits. "Just organization. Hey, come on"—he showed us an expanse of perfect teeth and slopped Scotch into our glasses—"come on, everybody. This is a celebration. You got the consignment here in one piece, and the Javits Corp.'s real proud of you." He clapped Stanno encouragingly across the shoulders with a blanched and freckled hand. Stan gave him an ingenuous grin—which was a lot more than I could have managed in his shoes.

"What's happening to those two of Brückner's bunch that we've got locked up?" asked Selby. Javits shrugged.

"Nothing, I guess. They're probably grateful to be alive. What with being illegal immigrants here, most likely without passports and having been involved in a piracy deal, I doubt if they'll make any static."

"You don't think they'll get in touch with Anscudden?"

"Hell, no; why should they? They've failed and that's it. What's he to them, anyway?"

"Same as he was to Brückner," I said: "an outdated old cipher. Just nobody loves Anscudden."

"Hoo boy, wait till Demirel turns up in Tripoli with those Israeli boxes," said Javits; "then watch his stock drop right out of the market."

"Talking of finance," I said to him, "you owe my mates the other half of their money. Me, I don't mind if you want to add mine to my salary."

"Ah yes, money." Javits tapped his teeth with a fingernail. "Money. Of course." He paused. "Look, gentlemen," he said, "there's still something I'd like done. . . ."

"We've done what we agreed to do," broke in Stanno. "Now we get paid as arranged."

"I understand your concern, gentlemen," said Javits, addressing a spot somewhere up among the rafters, "but if you'll cast your minds back, I think you'll recall we agreed that you undertook to neutralize the threat to my cargo from Anscudden and his accomplices. That threat still exists, although feebly. Mr. Selby, here, has kindly suggested that he sail with the *Trebizond* and stay aboard at least as far as Gibraltar to keep an eye on things and to soothe Captain Ratnayaka's—uh—qualms with small gifts. So he'll be getting the rest of his money a bit later than planned. Similarly, there's one small thing I'd like to ask of you and your friend, Lee." Javits turned to me. "It's very simple."

"Go ahead."

"For my own reasons, I want you to fetch Mr. Anscudden here. He's got the answers to some questions that have been bothering me for a long time. Only thing is, I can't ask him in person. I'll be honest with you, I don't want him knowing it's me asking the questions. Later on it wouldn't matter a damn, but right now it'd be kinda awkward. So if you'd like to get the guy here, I'll give you a list of questions to put to him. I don't give a fart in a bottle how you get him to answer them, but you know the man too and I reckon you'll be able to judge when you're getting the truth."

"I don't follow you, Mr. Javits," I said, baffled, "but I suppose as I'm on the payroll . . ."

"You don't have to understand it," said Javits belligerently; "you just have to do it." I had no idea why he wanted Anscudden questioned or why he should suddenly have adopted this manic tone.

"You're calling the shots," I told him pacifically. "I just thought I'd make a better job of it if I knew exactly what I was doing."

Poor Stan was clearly in a quandary. Not getting paid on the nail bothered him, I knew, but perhaps he'd be willing to defer that for a day or two in exchange for settling scores with Anscudden in person. He was obviously worried about Selby going off alone with the cargo of guns. He didn't trust Selby as I did, because he hardly knew him, but he was in no position to raise objections without telling Javits that we were after his shipment. There was a brief pause while he came to the same conclusion.

"Okay," he said finally. "I think it's a pretty fast one you've pulled, Mr. Javits, but you seem to be holding all the aces."

Javits nodded his great ginger-and-white head. "Thank you, gentlemen," he said. "I guess that's settled. I leave the rest to you."

12

The *Trebizond* sailed at three o'clock on Monday morning. Stanno and I sat on a bollard on the wharf and watched as Captain Demirel slipped his cables. Practically as soon as the wash from its screws had stopped gurgling round the wooden piling below us, its sister ship, with Ratnayaka at the helm, took its place, and the cranes once more swung into operation. It was a freakishly warm night for the time of year, and I was tired; for a while I just sat and watched the water creeping up the *Marmara*'s Plimsoll line as she settled under the weight of the Czech arms.

Selby had been standing on the bridge watching the loading. Now he came down the gangway and joined us.

"Sixteen million dollars," he said, nodding towards the open hatches with the quivering cables being lowered into them.

"I still want to know when I shall get my hands on some of it," growled Stanno tensely. Apart from his doubts about Selby, I reminded myself, he was still a deserter on the run and hence under additional strain. I hoped Selby would think of that before he lost his cool. I needn't have worried, of course.

"Look, old man," he said, "I know how you feel. But you've got a job to do with Lee, here, so you can't come with me. Not unless you want to leave your ten grand behind?"

Stanno remained staring motionlessly out across the harbor.

"Okay, then," resumed Selby. "It'll all be as we planned. When I've got the stuff, I'll meet you both in London, because I'll need Lee's know-how in order to get rid of it at the best price. If I take it to a fence in a hurry, the sixteen million will get whittled away to less than ten—perhaps even less than eight. We'll make a proper job of it. But meanwhile, I'll have got it safe. I know you think I might rat on you," he said to Stan, "but if you use your brain for a moment, you'll realize that if I did, you could finger me to the CIA or the Tanzanians or even Javits himself. My life wouldn't be worth living with that crowd after me."

This seemed to convince Stan, who cheered up to the extent of going back into the warehouse and getting slightly drunk on Javits' whisky. So the night wore away into dawn, but it was getting on for nine o'clock before the exhausted Maltese dockers fetched out the last pallet of crates. Captain Ratnayaka had come down and was standing on the wharf glaring moodily at the streaky patches of rust on the *Marmara*'s side.

"I do not like this," he said as he caught sight of me. "I do not like this at all." He looked dead tired, and I thought he had probably not slept since leaving Trieste.

"So you keep saying, Captain."

"There is something wrong. The *Trebizond* was chartered to go to Tanzania. Then Mr. Javits changes his mind and tells me to go to Malta. I do not mind his changing his mind, but now I have to change my ship. Very good—Mr. Javits

113

is paying, and it is his cargo, I think. But . . ."

"For God's sake, don't pull this naive crap on me," I interrupted wearily. "You're an experienced seaman, Ratnayaka, and you're in charge of a scrubby little freighter flying a flag of convenience. Perhaps you think you really are legit, but it's time you got over it. What the hell do you think is in those crates? What the hell do you think's going into your hold right now? You're a gunrunner, Captain, and don't forget it."

"I'm not a fool, Mr. Lee—or Mr. Kowalski, or whoever you call yourself today . . ."

"It's Lee on Mondays."

". . . Mr. Lee. I'm not a fool, and neither was I born yesterday. But six people were killed aboard my ship in the last two days. I thought I too would die. I want to know what to be expecting."

I sighed. "You mean more money?"

"We'll come to terms with that on the way," said Selby soothingly. He had moved across from watching the hatches battened.

Ratnayaka perked up a bit at that, I thought, rather as if he'd wanted Selby to commit himself in front of witnesses. I couldn't understand the fuss he was making. Pompous Asiatic git, trying to pull that wet-behind-the-ears bullshit. What he wanted was more lucre. Well, don't we all, so why couldn't he say so? The crafty sod just thought he could screw more out if he hammed it up a bit. A man of principle, my ass. Half an hour later, the Captain took the *Marmara* out round Senglea Point into Grand Harbour, doubtless with Selby standing beside him up on the bridge fortifying him with glimpses of banknotes.

Stanno and I took a cab into town to find somewhere to sleep. I for one was too tired to do any more thinking. Stan fell asleep in the taxi and was not looking his best when we arrived at a pension that looked suitably anonymous.

"We want a bed," I told the fat woman lovingly dusting a rubber plant in the tiled hall. She looked at us.

"A double one?" she inquired frostily.

"Not necessarily," I said. "It's sleep we're after. You know, tired travelers."

She looked us over again, and whatever she thought she saw she obviously didn't go a bundle on. I signed the book, giving my home address as Darmstadt, and showed her my passport. When I nudged him, Stanno drowsily produced his, but had to glance surreptitiously at his new first name on the inside page before signing in.

"You have no luggage," the woman observed acutely.

"That's right," I said. "Our plane crashed and we lost everything, so the Red Cross gave us your address. They said yours was the warmest welcome in town."

She sniffed and palmed the ten bucks I folded and pushed her way. I took the keys she offered and we made for the stairs.

"You have separate rooms," she called after us. "We do not allow men together in a single room in this house. There are other hotels for that purpose. This is a family pension." We went on climbing the stairs. "And no visitors permitted upstairs," she added.

"I bet she thinks her relationship with that rubber plant's just platonic," I said to Stanno, but I don't think he heard me. I got him into his room and left him there. Then I put myself to bed, knowing that I ought to be doing something about Anscudden but being unable to remember what the hell it was.

When I woke, it was to find the room in semidarkness. I looked at my watch: ten past six. I had slept the entire day away. I lay back and thought how little my bedroom lived up to the bourgeois promise of the tiled entrance hall. It was a dismal box of hardwood partitions which had holes gouged in them plugged with screws of lavatory paper. My next-door neighbor was noisily expending his energy just the other side of the partition. The wood was split up by thin lines of yellow light where the panels joined, and it would have taken a much less curious person than I to ignore the possibilities. I rolled wearily over on the hard mattress and its thin grayish sheet and applied my eye to the nearest crack.

Not two feet away was an expanse of pink flesh covered with a pelt of black hair. The hairs shifted sideways abruptly as the guy sat back on his haunches, and I could see that he was quite young—only about twenty probably, but it's not always easy to judge with Mediterranean types. He was covered all over with the hairs, and the naked bulb hanging from the ceiling overhead made the sweat on them shine. The girl lying back with the inside of her thighs clasping his hips was also young—probably two or three years younger. She didn't look like a whore. They were probably a couple of lovers who found this the easiest way of getting round the strict Catholic conventions that made it practically impossible ever to be alone with somebody in Malta unless you were married. She had her feet locked behind the small of his back, and I noticed that her toenails were painted the color of dried blood. She was screwing up her toes rhythmically, and although she wasn't moving about on the bed, her stomach heaved a little as if movement were taking place inside.

Evidently it had a rapid effect, for a look of either pure agony or pleasure fixed the boy's face in a snarl and he tried to pull away from her, jerking out some words in Maltese. I remembered old Stanno in Dubrovnik and wondered if this guy was saying the same thing. With a desperate heave he managed to get himself free of her, but only in the nick of time. The girl was watching intently, holding her head up from the pillow, her mouth opened very wide, ready to take his as he sank forward onto her in temporary exhaustion, shuddering. I wished them both well, even to the extent of hoping that if they stuck together for any time they would broaden their repertoire. Pleasant enough as it was, no doubt, but all a bit straight. Strictly for school kids. Still, so much for the family-style pension.

Suddenly I remembered what I had failed to do before going to bed. I had to wire Anscudden in case he was about to fly to Tripoli to meet the *Trebizond*. On the way downstairs I looked in at Stanno, but he was still asleep. The fat woman wasn't in the hall, but I heard a noise and glanced over the reception desk to find a small child in pajamas sitting on the floor eating spaghetti from a bowl with his fingers. He looked up at me, his mouth frozen open in mid-chew and rimmed with tomato sauce. It was hard to realize that in a dozen years he'd be doing what was going on upstairs.

I went out and found a post office and sent a cable to Anscudden c/o the British Consulate, Palermo. It read:

117

PROBLEMS STOP MEET HERE SOONEST HOTEL BRISTOL STOP BRUCKNER. Not as scholarly as he was accustomed to, no doubt, but I thought he'd find it compelling enough. Then I looked through the phone book to check the address of the hotel where an Israeli friend of mine had once died of food poisoning, leaving me a Czech Model 52 pistol.

The proprietor recognized me immediately, for all that I'd grown one of those droopy moustaches since we'd last met.

"Still working for Mr. Javits?" he asked when we had gone through the long-time-no-see ritual. I swear that man knows everything that happens in Malta and quite a lot of what goes on outside, too.

"Still am, Bill," I said. "I'm a loyal Corporation man. At least, during office hours."

"I hear such things about Mr. Javits," said Bill, scratching his head. "As you are not in your office now, I can tell you that people here say he's a bit mad."

I laughed. "I expect they're right, but it's a profitable madness. Anyway, to hell with Javits. I'm on a job, Bill, and I don't want to use Corporation facilities. Can you get me a couple of handguns?"

"Sure, Mr. Lee. What you want?"

"Nothing expensive. I need them to wave rather than shoot with. I've got some persuading to do."

"Auto?"

"It doesn't matter." I gave him two hundred dollars.

"Okay. You wait here ten minutes."

He was back in eight with a brown carrier bag. "One's not much," he said apologetically, "but they both *look* like guns. And they're not hot."

I nodded and unwrapped the two oil-stained bundles

inside. The first was a nearly mint Turkish job, a Kirikkale. It's a copy of the Walther PP with a couple of minor changes of detail, chambered for .38 ACP. A perfectly respectable eight-shot automatic with a four-inch barrel and black plastic handgrips.

"How much?" I asked Bill. I knew it would fetch slightly under ninety dollars if imported new into the U.S.

"A hundred and ten," he said. I nodded again. Malta isn't the States.

The other gun was a beat-up Spanish job, a 9mm Astra Condor. I checked the action and barrel. It wasn't a booby trap, but it had certainly been around.

"Fifty?" suggested Bill hopefully.

"Okay," I said. "And keep the change. They'll do fine."

"Thank you, Mr. Lee. That's very kind. Here." He produced a couple of small boxes of ammunition from a coat pocket. "I have some bullets. But not many."

"We won't need many," I said. I checked the caliber before I turned to go.

"You have not forgotten that your friend left his passport here, Mr. Lee?" Bill reminded me on my way out. "I have kept it for you here. I knew you would come back, you see." He unlocked a tiny safe and produced the passport that had been on the body: a Dutch one, very worn, in the name of van der Meersch. Haym's picture stared back at me from the first page. I flicked through the rest. It was full of visas for places like Iceland. I wondered what had taken him there; he had mostly been working on Nazis who had gone off to Egypt to help Nasser with his rockets or his press. Many less-justifiable ways of expending one's meager allowance of years.

119

"Keep it," I said to Bill, handing it back. "Do what you like with it. It'll come in handy someday and get some poor sod out of a hole."

In exchange I took a timetable of flight arrivals into Luqa airport that he had on the counter.

"Why don't you stay in my hotel, Mr. Lee?" he asked.

"No offense, Bill," I said, tapping the passport I had returned to him. "But look what happens to people who do."

I went back to the pension, picking up a razor on the way. Stanno was up and dressing when I looked in.

"It's a bloody knocking shop, this place," he said, pulling on a sock.

"I know. Don't worry, we'll report them to the Michelin Guide. That'll knock the bottoms out of their trade."

"Christ knows why you have to go and choose somewhere like this. With the money in our pockets we could have had a suite in the Hilton."

We shaved and went out for something to eat. I took the timetable along and looked up the flights from Palermo. Assuming that Anscudden had just about received the cable, we saw that the earliest he could arrive in Malta was three o'clock tomorrow afternoon. Bearing in mind that the *Trebizond* should be arriving at midnight tonight, I also noticed that the only flight from Tripoli on a Tuesday got into Luqa two hours and five minutes after the plane I expected Anscudden to be on. If everything decided to happen at once tomorrow, it looked as if it might turn out to be a busy day.

13

In the morning, I went to Javits' suite in the Belvedere to collect the questions he wanted me to ask Anscudden. I glanced at them briefly: a typed list of nine queries—some more or less intelligible; others little more than a single word followed by a question mark.

"Look," I said, "what the hell is all this? None of these make any sense to me." I waved the typescript.

"Just some points he can help me clear up," said Javits. "It's no good pushing me, Lee; I'll explain when I'm good and ready."

Somehow there was a secretiveness, almost a furtiveness, that was out of character. Usually Javits was honest with me even when being discreet. This scheming was new, and I didn't like it. I couldn't see the point in his laying down the rules without telling me what the game was called.

"You're sure Anscudden'll understand these?" I asked.

"He'll understand," said Javits. "If he doesn't, he's not trying hard enough. If he's not trying hard enough, it'll be because you've gone soft."

"He's not all mush himself," I said, thinking of Aden.

"Aw, come on; he went to one of those sassy schools you British are so proud of. I forget the name."

"Think of him as an Old Nuneatonian," I said.

"Uh-huh. When do you think he'll get in?"

"There's a flight from Palermo this afternoon."

Javits nodded. "You'll need somewhere he can make a bit of noise. I'd take him down to the warehouse. The men'll have finished by twelve."

"Finished what?"

"We're pulling out of Malta," said Javits. "I've decided. I'll tell you about it later. At the moment I've got about a hundred guys busting guts to ship the stuff back to Trieste. Malta and the Javits Corp. don't like each other anymore; they don't trust each other's security."

"Okay." Well, that was his business. It only seemed screwy because it was so sudden. "There's only one thing," I told him, taking the key Javits was holding out: "I'm going to need a car. You got one I could use?"

"Sure do," he said. "There's a rental company we have an account with. Choose what you want and charge it. I'll call 'em up."

"Thanks."

"When you're through, I'll be right here."

Five hours later, Stanno and I watched the three-o'clock Alitalia Caravelle from Palermo touch down at Luqa. We looked absurd in dark glasses and a couple of plastic rain caps, but I didn't think Anscudden would recognize us until it was too late to do anything about it. It was impossible to describe my feelings as I saw him come through the Customs hall carrying an attaché case. He looked every inch the young ex-officer: tall and slim and obviously carefully dressed, so that there seemed to be a lot of clean edges cutting him away from whatever background he chose to stand against. He had lost some of his blondish hair; otherwise he looked pretty much as I remembered. I sensed Stanno beside me stiffen.

"Right," I said to him. "Go and sit in the car. We'll play it as arranged." I turned to the Maltese porter I had just given ten dollars. "The tall, fair one," I said, nodding.

"Okay, mister." The porter bustled up to Anscudden and removed his attaché case from his grip with practiced ease. "Taxi, sir—I gotta best taxi in Malta. Where you wanna go, sir?" He pushed with the case against the chest of a genuine taxi driver, letting off a short burst of Maltese. "He no good, sir; his taxi it always break. My taxi the best in Malta. . . ."

Anscudden, the gentleman, was no match for this. He allowed himself to be propelled outside and into the passenger seat of the hire car, a crimson Fiat. Before he could come to his senses, I climbed in behind the wheel, and we took off.

"You can take me to the Hotel Bristol," Anscudden said breathlessly.

"And you can learn to say 'please.' It's a word you're going to need, mate, believe me." He looked sharply sideways at me.

"I really don't think I need lessons in manners from you," he said in those frosty tones which reawakened old memories. "Your job is to drive this taxi to the Hotel Bristol." Something about the setup must have struck him as wrong then, for he peered closely at me again and reached for his door handle. The muzzle of Stanno's Turkish automatic rammed into the back of his neck.

"Your job," I pointed out to him, "is to see if you can stay alive. You start practicing right now."

There was a short silence while the Fiat tore along the road. We were already practically into Tarxien.

"Who are you?" Anscudden asked.

"Just someone who's advising you to put both hands on the dash where my friend can see them," I said. "Your time's running out." Hastily he leaned forward and placed his hands on the facia. I pulled off my plastic cap and dropped it on the floor. "Do you have a gun?"

"No."

"If you're lying, you're a dead man, Anscudden." There was another silence. We were through Tarxien and Pawla. We forked right towards Cospicua.

"Don't I know you?" he asked me. He was unable to keep the anxiety out of his voice. I flashed him a mirthless smile.

"We met in the Army, *Major*. You remember the dear old Regiment out in Aden? You remember the testing ranges on Salisbury Plain? The name's McGundrell, and the fellow with the pistol behind you is Stanno. Just now we're not taking you to a reunion dinner."

"It wouldn't be the same without Micky Cullen," explained Stanno from the back.

Anscudden had gone very pale, and when he shifted his hands nervously on the black plastic, I saw the sweaty outline his fingers left.

"*Quite* still," I said, and Stanno rammed the muzzle in harder above his impeccable white collar. Anscudden drew in his breath sharply.

The road was remarkably empty, and we made good time. I took the left-hander down to French Creek, and in a minute we reached the wharf. The iron gates were locked, and behind them the quay was empty. The giant crane sat on its rails, hook swinging slowly in the cold breeze. Already the gray late-afternoon sky was beginning to darken; outlined against it, a few gulls sat perched on top of the warehouse with its white capitals: Z. GRECH. I parked the car and switched off.

"You're going to kill me," said Anscudden, as if he dared not turn it into a question.

"Maybe. We might not be awfficers and gentlemen, but we're not common assassins." Even as I said it, I wondered if there was such a thing as a common assassin; they'd always seemed a rare breed to me. Anscudden looked slightly relieved, which was what I had hoped. There are more ways of softening meat than by hitting it with a steak hammer. I reached over and took his attaché case. It wasn't locked. In it were a few overnight things in a pigskin folder with a zip, a bottle of something expensive to dab on the smelly parts and a copy of *Time.* "Out," I said. "Slowly."

He climbed stiffly out, and I produced the Astra, whose battered muzzle I waved at him while Stanno frisked him. He was clean.

"You've just bought yourself some more time," I said. I found the key and unlocked the padlock on the iron gates. I was glad I'd got it from Javits; climbing in would have been no joke. The right-hand gatepost extended down into the dark waters of the harbor, and some thoughtful soul had constructed a sort of fan of steel spikes over the water to discourage trespassers from swinging themselves around the post. On the other side, the left-hand gate was hung from a post that was sunk into a wall as high as itself— about twelve feet, as far as I could judge. The wall was brick and sheer: no handholds anywhere; and the iron-spike artist had done his bit there as well with a lot of short spines set in a long revolving rowel.

125

Stanno motioned Anscudden through the gate with his gun, and I followed. There was not a soul about. Ahead of us stretched the deserted quay; across its cobbled surface a few loose wood shavings were rolling aimlessly before the breeze. To our right lay the harbor; to our left was the huge bulk of the warehouse, with the Corradino Heights rising steeply behind it. The main sliding doors were locked and barred. We marched Anscudden round to the far end, where the access door was. Because it had been nighttime when the *Trebizond* berthed, I'd never noticed there was a back entrance to the quay as well. Evidently a road ran the length of the wharf behind the warehouse, fenced off by balks of heavy timber set on end and much overgrown with prickly-pear. A couple of sheets of rusty corrugated iron were leaning casually up against the fence; glancing behind them, I discovered a gap a few feet across. Maybe security wasn't all that wonderful, at that.

I unlocked the side door and stepped in over the ledge, switching on the main overhead lights. Stanno and Anscudden followed me in and stood there. The first thing I noticed was how much warmer it was in than out; the second, that it had been stripped bare. The deep bays formed by huge piles of crates had vanished; gone were the stacks of ammunition boxes. There were only some splintered slats of wood lying about, together with some torn sacking. The place was empty. Nothing but the lingering scent of gun oil in the air. I reached up and clicked the switches that turned on the lights in the inner building that had served as Javits' office and armory; being inside the warehouse itself, this separate section had no ceiling to it. On impulse I switched off the main lights, so that what light there was in the warehouse came only from inside this office. It streamed yellowly up towards the distant steel girders over-head that supported the high tin roof. Enough light was reflected back down again to throw the rest of the building into a gloomy relief of littered floor and deep shadow.

I led the way into the brightly lit office, our footsteps gritting and echoing on the concrete. Inside, the high wooden gun racks had been emptied. All that was left was the heavy wooden workbench with a vise clamped to one end and a table with a chair standing on it.

"Go and find some rope," I told Stanno. We could hear him moving about the warehouse, and then he reappeared with an assortment of wire, lashings and binder twine.

"What are you going to do?" asked Anscudden nervously.

"Tie you up and ask you some questions, that's all," I said.

"Oh, there's no need to tie me up," he said with an attempt at a laugh whose hollowness was amplified by the tinny echoes. "I'm not going anywhere. I'll tell you anything you want. I've no secrets."

Without speaking, Stanno pushed Anscudden's chest with the muzzle of his gun, backing him until his calves came up against the edge of the chair, which I'd set down on the floor. Anscudden sat very suddenly, looking frightened and alert. I helped Stanno tie his hands and feet, and then we lashed the chair firmly back against the empty gun racks.

"Okay, Stan," I said, "you can leave him to me. Go and keep a lookout on the quay. If anyone turns up, come and tell me; don't start shooting because we might find you'd knocked off my boss."

"Right," he said. "But if you have any trouble with this bastard"—he kicked Anscudden's shin contemptuously—"one through the roof'll bring me right in." He walked off through the shadows, and we heard the side door close. The echoes died away.

I walked over and hitched myself onto the corner of the table, looking musingly at my trussed victim for a full minute. His pale, manic eyes stared back puzzledly. Finally, he couldn't stand it any longer.

"What's all this for?" he blurted out, adding foolishly, "I've got someone to see at five o'clock."

I gave him another minute's silence while I wondered why he hadn't put up more resistance. He seemed numbed. Perhaps all that effortless superiority had slowed him down. That's the trouble with his class: they forget what to do in emergencies because they're used to all that insulation of privilege cushioning the blows. With great deliberation, I cocked the Astra and found that the worn old mechanism made a satisfyingly menacing sound.

"This can be very quick," I said, "depending on you." Anscudden's tongue came out and licked his lips.

"Good God, man," he said. "You can't just execute me."

"I want answers to some questions. I'm not giving you explanations or chat. I just want answers, and I want them fast. If I think you're lying, I'm going to turn you over to Stanno. He's a killer, you know, and he's fresh from Ulster. He remembers Micky Cullen, too. Okay"—I pulled Javits' typed list from my pocket and put the pistol down on the table—"here comes number one. Your starter for nine. Who was Sauer's and your contact at the Lagos High Commission?"

"Jesus!" Anscudden's eyes widened.

"He was not." I picked up the gun, hitched myself off the table, walked over to him and cracked the barrel across the bridge of his nose. His eyes filled with tears, and he hung his head, a thick worm of blood inching out of his right nostril.

"Fer . . . Ferringer," he whispered.

"Louder."

"Ferringer."

"Spell it." He did, and I wrote it down opposite the question. "Number two: who chartered the DC–6?"

"Rigby-Smith."

"Three: the Combine's account number in the Zürich Handelsbank?"

"J-7003158."

I leaned over and pressed my thumb on the swelling on the top of his nose, feeling the bone pulpy beneath. He tried to pull away and shake it off, but I grabbed the side of his face with my spare fingers. He screamed.

"FJ-70031582. It's true—I swear to God it's true."

I wiped my thumb on his shirtfront and went back to the table and wrote busily.

"That was the one I really wanted to know," I told him. "I don't much care about the others, so I'm now going to shoot you through the right ear." I picked up the gun again.

"Anything!" shouted Anscudden, straining against the ropes. "Ask me anything you like, Mr. McGundrell. Please. I'll tell you."

"Corporal to you."

"Corporal McGundrell. Just ask," he pleaded.

" 'Damascus 1970,' " I read out. " ' Details.' "

At the end of a quarter of an hour, there were written answers beside six of Javits' questions. I was dragging from Anscudden secrets whose revelation, we both knew, would break him forever in the business and would probably cost him his life. In their place went fear: partly the awareness

129

of what would happen when he was caught up with, but mostly the immediate fear of what I was going to do first. His face was wet with tears and blood, and as his panic increased, so his replies were becoming more difficult to hear.

"I'm not enjoying this," I told him conversationally; "it gives me no pleasure. I just don't care, that's all. So far as I'm concerned, you're expendable. Quite apart from murdering Micky, what we saw you do in the Crater put you outside the right to be considered as a human being with the same value as everyone else. Sometimes at night I can still see that Arab girl you stuck that cane of yours into. She was only a kid, and you damn well knew she hadn't sheltered so much as a goat, let alone four guerrillas on the run."

"We had a job to do," whispered Anscudden. "I had orders."

"So do I have a job to do," I said, "and I have orders too. The only difference is I don't get a bang out of carrying them out to the limits of my imagination."

By the time we had finished number eight, Anscudden was broken. By keeping up the pressure, I had managed to make him further oscillate between terror and resignation, and finally he'd become confused. Apart from breaking his nose, I had, in fact, used very little physical coercion. The right combination of threats and bullying had been sufficient to reduce him to a state in which I knew he was telling the truth. He could no longer lie; he could no more resist complying than he had been able to when, as an outranked cadet, he had once unlocked the school armory to the IRA.

I picked up the pistol and tapped the question paper with the muzzle.

"Last one, Anscudden," I said, frowning at the three typed words. "Frankly, it's pretty bizarre, but it's a one-word answer. So pull yourself . . ."

Stanno came in very fast and quiet. He stood in the doorway, his gun loosely held and pointing at the floor.

"We've got visitors," he said. "Two of them. Have you finished?"

"Pretty well. Opposition?"

"Can't tell; it's too dark. They're casing the place."

"Let's get out." I checked I had left nothing behind. Anscudden seemed too confused to care what was happening. Then, as Stanno and I turned to go, we heard the echoing click of the warehouse door being opened. Silently we eased our way out of the office and moved in the opposite direction, hugging the partition wall. We dodged round behind the far corner and stood there, guns in our hands. There was a pause while they stood and listened; then came the sound of footsteps crossing the warehouse floor, approaching the open office door with caution. A few yards to my right, a chink of yellow light showed in the wall, and for the second time in two days I was the witness of something not intended for others' eyes.

One was thin and tall, probably in his late twenties; the other was older and shorter, with a round face and a complexion like the surface of a plate of porridge. Both were dark. They stood in the doorway looking silently at Anscudden. The thin one said something to his colleague in a language I didn't understand.

"Anscudden!" said the shorter man sharply. Anscudden looked up at him blearily. "I am Brigadier Shwedi, and this is Colonel Muftah Hanesh. In Libya, *hanesh* means 'snake,'" he added conversationally.

Anscudden nodded blankly. I could see him trying to come to terms with a changed situation.

"We are here at the express command of the Revolutionary Council," went on Shwedi. "How you come to be in these circumstances does not concern us. Frankly, I suppose some of your many enemies must have caught up with you. We've not come for explanations or excuses; our duty is to carry out a sentence. But I too went to Sandhurst, so as another officer I will give you a single chance to justify yourself. Where are the guns you promised us?"

Anscudden blinked. Both his eyes were turning black as a result of his broken nose.

"In . . . in the *Trebizond*," he croaked.

"You sent the consignment now aboard the *Trebizond*?" asked Shwedi, as if he wanted to make it quite clear. Anscudden nodded weakly.

"Then you have betrayed and insulted Libya," said Hanesh. "I hope you will agree that an officer is always to be held responsible for his actions."

Hanesh was holding a Beretta 951—a nicely made nine-mil job and the standard service pistol of the UAR, which was maybe how he'd got it. He now laid this on the table and dragged the heavy workbench over in front of Anscudden. Then he produced a pocketknife and cut the ropes that held Anscudden's hands. Anscudden flexed his fingers, wincing, then gingerly touched the bridge of his nose with a fingertip. Hanesh meanwhile had found some more pieces of cord and made a slipknot in the ends of two lengths. He removed Anscudden's coat, picked up his unresisting hands and tightened a knot around each wrist. Then he stretched out both cords across the bench top and over the far edge,

132

tying them to the legs of the bench so that both Anscudden's arms were pulled tautly out in front of him.

I knew what was coming then, and I think Anscudden did too. He began whimpering as Hanesh dragged back his shirt sleeves and knotted a piece of twine very tightly round each forearm. Shwedi produced a sheet of paper which he handed to his colleague. Colonel Hanesh stood smartly to attention with his back to the table at which Javits had served us whisky. He held the paper in his left hand, and from where I was I could see it was divided into two columns of type; presumably the Arabic original was on the right and the English translation on the left. He cleared his throat.

" 'The Revolutionary Council of the Revolutionary Islamic Government of the Libyan people has unanimously found Timothy Anscudden guilty in his absence of the crime of theft from the said Libyan people. With the express consent of Moammar Gaddafi, the Revolutionary Council has decreed that there is but one sentence which may be passed, and this it has empowered Brigadier Hamdullah Shwedi to carry out.' "

Anscudden had been watching numbly as Hanesh was reading, still whimpering and sniffing. Now he fell abruptly silent as if mesmerized, for from inside his jacket Shwedi produced a heavy-bladed butcher's knife. He stepped over to Anscudden and laid the flat of the blade across his right wrist, saying a phrase of Arabic softly as he did so. As the metal touched his skin, Anscudden began a long, terrible scream which filled the empty building and rang around the tin roof. Then Shwedi raised the knife and, with a single thudding blow, severed Anscudden's hand.

133

Now that it came to it, I found my attitude to Anscudden's fate was by no means as indifferent as I had told him. The situation was ironic: since the Army I had never thought of him except with a cold feeling of hatred uppermost. There was a whole imbalance that needed redressing: the torturing of Arab civilians, the murder of my friend, the relentless victimization and countless fatigues I'd suffered at his hands, the calculated taunts about class. For years I'd wished him dead, yet here he was being punished for an act we had committed for him. In a curious way, it didn't seem right; it was an unwarranted intrusion into a private matter by two outsiders.

The screaming had subsided to a continuous high-pitched stumbling babble like a twelve-inch disk played at 45 rpm. This sound gradually gave way to moans and snuffling. To my right, Stanno had his eye glued to a split in the wall. I snatched a glance through my own aperture and saw that Anscudden's right arm now ended in a pulpy red stump. Despite the twine that bit deeply into the skin of his forearm, a spreading pool of blood was forming under the blunt end. On the edge of the table under his nose lay his white and bloodless hand, its fingers slightly curled.

Hanesh had begun reading from the script again in his unemotional voice. He sounded like a policeman giving evidence.

" 'Secondly, the Revolutionary Council of the Revolutionary Islamic Government of the Libyan people has unanimously found Timothy Anscudden guilty in his absence of deception and insult towards Islam; namely, the substitution of Israeli boxes containing sand in the place of a promised consignment. The Revolutionary Council has

134

unanimously decreed that the aforementioned crimes of deception and insult compound and exacerbate the grave crime of theft from the said Libyan people and cannot remain unpunished. Hence, the second sentence unanimously agreed upon by the Revolutionary Council is held by that Council to have exemplary as well as punitive force for the instruction of all who may be tempted to hold the Revolutionary Libyan people's movement in contempt. The sentence is the same as the first, namely . . .' "

Here Hanesh's impassive voice was drowned by another scream, consisting of a crescendo of the word "No" shouted as fast as despair could articulate it.

" 'The Revolutionary Council,' " Hanesh could be heard saying in his precise way, " 'has once more empowered Hamdullah Shwedi to carry out sentence.' "

"Oh, no, no! *No!* Jesus Christ, no, not again! No, God, no, not the other one. Please, I beg you, I beseech you, no-o-o . . ." Distorted by pain and shouting, the voice soared beyond comprehensibility.

Shwedi still held the heavy knife. Its blade was wet with blood, which was beginning to form into dark streaks, as blood does before it clots. The blood had also run down onto Shwedi's hand and wrist, but it didn't seem to bother him. Indeed, the little brigadier looked as cheerful as ever. It was the grin on his face that was really memorable, much more so than the knife he held.

Now Anscudden's face was thrown back, his eyes round and crazed, watching the grinning Shwedi as he approached with the knife. His mouth was a black O from which meaningless noises were squeezed by spasms of throat and lungs.

"I should add," said Hanesh flatly, "that this not torture.

135

It is justice." He shot a glance at his colleague, for whom the remark was doubtless as much intended as for the victim himself. Shwedi was clearly jarred by his subordinate's icy tone. He stepped quickly over to Anscudden and without hesitating chopped the knife's edge down on his left wrist with a short scrunching blow, following it with a lighter, trimming cut. This time Anscudden made no sound. His eyes had flickered up whitely in his head as he lost consciousness.

Hanesh stood up and refolded his piece of paper carefully before tucking it away in his inside pocket. He slipped the pistol into his waistband.

"*Qalas*," he said.

Shwedi had collected the severed hands together and now piled them neatly on top of the unconscious Anscudden's head. The fingers of the freshly amputated one were still trembling and twitching slightly and scrabbled at Anscudden's hair. Then, still holding the knife, he walked with his colleague towards the door.

"*Qalas*," he agreed.

I never was able to explain what happened next; at least, not satisfactorily. It was not the events that needed explanation—they were clear enough—but the motive that made Stanno step out from behind the wall as the Libyans were leaving, his gun in a two-handed grip. As he did so, he must have kicked something on the floor, for there was a slight metallic scraping such as a tin lid might have made. Hanesh was quick, I'll give him that; he'd probably trained with Al Fatah. He was dropping to a crouch even as he turned, and he and Stanno fired at much the same moment. Stan's bullet caught him in the side of the head, just above the ear. In that instant, frozen like a movie frame, I glimpsed the ballooning effect on the skull as the shock wave caused distension. Then Hanesh had fallen sideways to the floor.

Shwedi had been half out of the office and must have caught sight of me out of the corner of one eye. He swung his right arm with a backhanded sweep, but without taking aim. The butcher's knife sang past my head and went clattering off across the warehouse floor. The gesture had probably been as much to rid himself of it as to hit me, for his right hand was now free to go for his gun—which was, unfortunately, in his coat pocket. I fired carefully and hit him in the mouth.

It's a funny thing about blood coming from bullet wounds, because often the blood seems to *splash* out. This obviously couldn't be explained by blood pressure itself, because the heart hasn't anything like enough power unless a main artery is struck; it can only be the kinetic energy of the bullet's shock wave that blows blood out through the hole immediately the round has entered the body. A similar effect can be seen if you fire at plastic jugs of water with rounds designed to expand practically on contact. The water is mostly blown *forwards*, towards the shooter, through great gashes in the front of the jug, rather than backwards, as one might expect. It's an interesting phenomenon, and it was one of those things I noticed automatically because it was information I'd assimilated a long time ago. A great gout of blood leaped from Shwedi's mouth as the round struck him and he pitched over backwards.

Stanno was lying on his back near the corner of the wall, one leg doubled up underneath. It was the only time in my whole career when I'd seen a man shot exactly through the heart—except in front of a firing squad, of course. I squatted by the body and looked down at his face for a moment in the light that streamed out of the office into the black interior of the warehouse.

"What the hell did you have to go and do that for, Stan?" I asked, shaking my head. After a while I got up, ignoring the two Arabs, who I knew were going to stay down. I walked slowly back into the office.

Anscudden still sat at the workbench, firmly tied to his chair. He was unconscious, and although his head had lolled slightly sideways, he still wore the grotesque cap of his own hands. A trickle of blood had drained out of one of them and was worming its way over his forehead and down the side of his nose. There didn't seem much to be done, although I could feel my hatred melt away, to be replaced by a sort of benign distaste. Now he had so truly been cut down to size, he no longer loomed importantly on the landscape. He was just a balding ex-major who'd had his hands chopped off.

Suddenly his pale eyes opened. His face was gray.

"Fucked you up nicely, didn't they?" I observed, standing in front of him and watching his return to comprehension. He closed his eyes momentarily.

"Jesus, my hands hurt. My hands hurt."

I reached across the bench and removed his hands from the top of his head. I tossed them into a corner.

"They do?" I asked. He said nothing, but without warning suddenly vomited down his shirt and onto the bench. He appeared to have had some kind of spaghetti dish for lunch. "What a mess you're making of yourself," I commented. "I can't remember ever seeing an awfficer and a gentleman in such a mess."

"Please get me out of here," he said weakly, spitting. "I'll pay anything. Just get me to a hospital. Oh, God, my hands. They cut my hands off. *They cut my bloody hands off!*" His voice became a scream.

"That's bad," I said. "Just for the record, you did kill Cullen?"

His dropped gaze and silence were enough. I nodded slightly. Now I could see from the way one of his shirt sleeves had been dragged up that he was wearing cuff links with the crest of the Thanet Fusiliers, and he a man who had resigned his commission in order to make money in free enterprise. People like him want it both ways.

"You made a right cock-up with the Libyans, didn't you?" I said. Anscudden closed his eyes and then squeezed them tightly shut. I noticed that he was beginning to shiver with the onset of shock. He probably wouldn't last long without some sort of treatment.

"I don't understand," he whispered, "but I don't care anymore. I don't even want to know." Tears appeared under his eyelashes. The blood on his hair had clotted into a dark mat.

"You boobed. You were on the wrong side, Major; you were up against us."

"I . . . I came here to see Brückner."

"No, you didn't; I sent that cable. Brückner's on the seabed somewhere off Sicily. We rigged the whole thing."

There was a long silence. I thought for a moment he had fainted again or maybe died, and I went across to stare at his face. His raw stumps were beginning to clot, but fresh blood still oozed slowly onto the bench from both of them. He opened his eyes and blinked at me as if trying to remember who I was.

"Why?" he asked weakly. "Revenge?"

"No. Money."

Anscudden seemed to rally slightly, as if he had already experienced too much pain and terror to be capable of feeling anything more. He even managed the palest smile.

"Bad company," he whispered. "Bad company. They warned us about it at school."

"They just never told you how to spot it." I went and fetched Hanesh's pocketknife and cut the ropes that held him to the chair. He leaned forward and put the side of his face on the bench. Then slowly he began to bend his arms—which evidently hurt the stumps, because the wounds had begun to stick to the wood. He gave a soft scream and sat up, drawing his wounded arms to his chest for the first time. Although they had been free the moment Shwedi had cut his hands off, Anscudden had let them lie on the bench as if they were still tied or as if they no longer belonged to him. Then he looked once at the stumps of his own arms and began weeping hopelessly.

"I'm through now," I told him. "For your information, those two maniacs are dead. So is my friend Stanno. I don't feel like hanging around. I'll maybe call an ambulance when I get back into town."

Slowly he shook his head, sniffing.

"I've had enough," he whispered. "I've never really enjoyed any of it. You'll be doing me a favor if you finish it."

"You're sure about that?" I asked. He looked at me and nodded. Surprising even myself, I simply bent forward and cut the twine that bound his forearms. At first the blood seeped unwillingly through the crushed arteries, but soon the flow became more rapid. Anscudden sighed and leaned forward again, resting his head on the bench.

"Oh, shit," I said; "hold on a moment. I've forgotten there's still another fucking question." I found the crumpled list in my pocket. "Just remember," I told him, "it's not me who wants to know this but a real screwball. Question number nine I've got here reads: 'Do you repent?' "

He made no sound, but lay there without moving while his life ran out of the ends of his arms and over the edge of the bench. After a time, I left him there and walked out of the warehouse, pausing only to take from Hanesh's body the script he'd read out. As I left, I turned off the office lights. Darkness descended behind me. It wasn't very much lighter outside, although it was still only early evening. I could just make out the black lattice work of the crane boom sticking up at the end of the quay. A small boat was puttering across the harbor, the white light on top of its mast pitching gently up and down. From somewhere on the other side, a man's shout floated out over the dark water. I took the Astra out of my pocket and tossed it into the harbor. It made a gentle splash. Then I walked out through the main gates, which I relocked behind me, got into the Fiat and drove away.

I went straight to Javits' suite, having scrubbed off as much blood as I could find on my hands with handkerchief and spit. I didn't perhaps look as suave as the typical Belvedere guest and drew a few unwelcoming stares in the foyer, but nobody stopped me—which was just as well for them. I was in no mood for explanations.

"I want a shower," I told Javits when he opened the door. He looked a bit taken aback—which was ridiculous, since he was the one wearing a gentian violet bathrobe made of some toweling material.

"Sure . . . uh . . . sure, Lee. Help yourself." At least he had the sense not to ask a lot of fool questions until I'd stood for ten minutes under a scalding stream of water. I reappeared feeling a whole lot cleaner externally.

"I've got your answers, in case you were worried," I told him. He handed me a chunky glass full of whisky.

"I knew you would, Lee."

"Stanno's dead," I said shortly, and I explained what had happened.

"I'm sorry about your friend," he said when I'd finished. "He was a bright kid. Tough shit those Arabs turning up. How in hell did they know where to go?"

"Captain Demirel must have told them where he loaded up," I said tiredly. "They certainly moved a lot faster than I expected. Oh, there is one thing. Halfway through chopping Anscudden up, one of them said something about Israeli boxes with sand in them. What happened to the Lee-Enfields?"

"Yeah," said Javits. "I got thinking while you were on your way from Trieste, those Lee-Enfields we bought could be traced back to us. Sure, toys change hands, but it would've been a hell of a coincidence for Anscudden to have got his on them at the right moment to pull the trick. Sand was a far better idea. Kind of an insult, if you think about it."

"That's how they took it." I gave Javits his crumpled list of answered questions. "He never got around to number nine," I said, "but I think the answer was no."

"Pity." He reached a white envelope off the desk behind him. "Thirty grand, Lee. That's a lot of money, but I reckon you earned every cent. Now I've got a small job I think you can handle."

"No."

"You're not thinking of retiring, are you?" Javits asked with concern. He ran a hand over his ginger hair.

"No. It's not enough for me to retire on. But I'm taking a break, Javits Corp. or no Javits Corp. I've got to get back to London for a few days."

"I'll tell you what, Lee," he said, picking up a slimmer envelope with MR. BECKERS on it. "Take a coupla weeks off, no questions asked, and then come on over to Vienna. There's something I want to discuss with you. Whether or not you go along with it, I'll have your friend's money waiting for you to collect."

"Just for coming to Vienna?"

"Just for that, Lee."

I sighed. "Okay, Mr. Javits. I'll be there. Perhaps you could then explain just what the hell I was doing tonight."

"Maybe."

"Meantime, there are a couple of things you can do. Number one, you can get me on a plane first thing in the morning to just about anywhere except Libya: I locked the warehouse, but I don't want to be around when it's unlocked. In any case, you can break in from the back, so I want out of Malta as soon as possible. Number two, you can get someone who knows his ass from his elbow to go over the Fiat for incriminating evidence; there may be blood."

Javits smiled his white-than-white smile. "I'm way ahead of you, Lee. You're booked to Rome in an hour and ten minutes: it's the last flight out tonight. Just grab your bag and go. Forget the car, I'll take care of that. If the story breaks, I think I can handle it."

"Thank God for the Javits Corporation," I said.

"I do," said Javits seriously. I turned to go. "And . . . uh . . . Lee. About that Swiss account number Anscudden gave you. I shouldn't bother; there's nothing in it."

14

It wasn't much of a holiday, as it happened, but at least a temporary sense of normality returned once I was back in London. Lee & Savernake looked as welcoming as I'd ever seen it, and Moleman had generated one of those fugs that small shopkeepers work up to counteract the cold blasts from the ever-opening door—an excuse that he didn't have.

In between catching up on business I gave him a blurred outline of what had happened, but even if I'd felt inclined to elaborate there would scarcely have been time, because within hours of arriving I was back at work. We had another visit from Chinde, the African who'd missed me earlier, and I found myself trying to negotiate a deal to supply some light machine guns to Frelimo, the Mozambique Liberation Front. I spent a lot of time in and around a couple of hotels off the Earls Court Road which were full of seedy killers from the ex-Colonies. They were a mixture of mercenaries and adventurers who sat about for months on end drinking beer and waiting for a phone call or telegram informing them that a nasty little rebellion had broken out somewhere. The ones who had fought in Katanga or Biafra were all very manic and getting a little old. One of them had a pouch for his cigarette lighter made from the scrotum of an African victim. Several of them wrote racist slogans on the walls of pub lavatories. It was a pleasure to get back to Blackheath at night.

Four days after I'd flown in, Malta hit the news in a big way, although this time it was nothing to do with Premier Mintoff. Dismal stringers in Sliema perked up out of the doze of their semiretirement and began phoning copy through to their London papers: more or less sensational accounts of what had been found in the Z. Grech warehouse. On the second day of the story, after they had successfully identified the mysterious Peder Beckers as a British soldier, I bought an Italian paper in Soho which was full of phrases like "indescribable scenes of torture," which it then proceeded to describe in detail. A British businessman had been "grievously mutilated" and, horrible discovery, his hands had been found lying in a corner of the warehouse, where they had been carelessly tossed. The police, concluded the story's last paragraph, were satisfied they knew the identity of the callous and bloodstained monster who had done the deed, and an arrest was imminent.

The *International Herald Tribune,* on the other hand, was more dispassionate—but none the wiser. The bodies at the warehouse had finally been identified as those of a British Army deserter, a British arms dealer and two Libyans traveling on false diplomatic papers. The story was that Stanno, the deserter, had been working for Anscudden on an unknown but undoubtedly shady deal when they had both fallen victim to the notoriously unscrupulous rivalry common in the twilit world of their sordid business. After a

145

couple more days, the story languished and died. Nothing approaching a real disclosure was made; Javits had been as good as his word.

Then one day I came home quite early, walking across the heath from the station. It was a misty November evening, about the time when you can see the violet glow of the early news on TV coming from behind people's curtains. Commuters' cars were headed for the suburbs, nose to tail, their headlights yellow. The air smelled of burned-out fireworks, and I had a feeling of well-being, even though the Frelimo deal was proving tricky. I climbed the stairs to my door, let myself in and found Selby sitting in a chair by the unlit fire. We looked at each other for a bit, and then I put down the pint of milk I was carrying.

"Sorry to break in," he said.

"Be my guest. Welcome home."

"I had to see you tonight, Lee. I tried phoning, but you were out. This seemed about the only way."

"I expect you know best," I told him.

There was an awkward pause while Selby produced a bottle of Scotch from his overcoat pocket and poured me a drink. I suppose if you're going to break into people's flats, you might as well bring your social graces along with you to tide you over the conversational flat spots.

"I read about Malta," he said. "Awful about old Stan. It sounded like a real fuck-up."

"More or less," I agreed, "except that Javits wound up with what he wanted, as usual. How about your end?"

"It didn't work out," he said. "I got off the *Marmara* at Gibraltar. It'll arrive in Dar early next week, I expect."

"Yes, I thought it might."

"Oh."

"I've got a brain," I said shortly, "and I've been using it these past ten days. I'd probably have cottoned on a lot earlier if there hadn't been so much going on."

"I see," said Selby. "How much have you worked out?"

"I don't know, but it feels like enough to me. It was too neat the way you went off alone with that bloody shipload of guns. You set the whole thing up, didn't you? Right from the beginning. In fact, I'd take a bet that it was you who deliberately leaked the news of the deal to the Libyans in the first place."

"Why would I do a silly thing like that?"

"Because you knew they wanted the arms themselves and would try a snatch. You wanted a genuine hijacking attempt to act as a diversion in case there'd been other leaks. You know what I think?"

"I've got a pretty good idea." Selby nodded sadly.

"I think it was you who arranged the original deal for Tanzania to buy Czech assault rifles with Agency funds. I don't know what kind of big wheel that makes you, but presumably you were told to ensure delivery at all costs. So to make certain, you decided to create a diversion to confuse any other attempts to steal the shipment—although as the Med's crawling with U.S. military, there was never any real chance of its going astray. However, to make sure of your diversion you needed two things. One of those was someone who could be guaranteed to keep the Libyans occupied. He'd also have to be someone you knew and could trust; so much the better if he was also involved in a phony plot with you to steal the guns, because that way you'd always be certain of knowing his actions in advance."

"Someone like you."

"Someone like me," I agreed. "Not just someone who could

be appealed to as a friend but also as a guy whose bank balance needed brightening up. I was the perfect sucker." Selby began to say something, but I held up a hand. "The other thing you needed to do in order to make the plan work," I went on, "was to brief Javits in case he took steps to screw up the Libyan hijacking attempt before it had even started. You told Javits the whole thing, right?"

"He knew, yes."

"So all that money he's been paying us isn't his at all; no wonder he was so generous with it. It was Agency money you *gave* him to finance a counterattack. He must've been busting a gut laughing when loyal old Lee McGundrell walked in right on time and volunteered his services."

"No more than you were, offering to protect his arms while planning to nick them yourself," said Selby. "It cuts both ways. Who was the deceiver and who the deceived?"

"Well, it bloody wasn't you, was it?" I said bitterly. "All the time, you were sitting outside and manipulating. Jesus, how could I have let myself fall for it?"

"I'm sorry, Lee," said Selby quietly; "I really am. I had to get you for the job, so I needed to make it as attractive as possible. I did have one stroke of luck, though, I'll admit: I knew from the moment those ex-Sandhurst Libyans chose Anscudden I could hook you. Before that I'd had my doubts."

"Screw you," I said. "That's what brought Stanno in, too; that and the money."

"I feel bad about him as well, Lee. But it needn't have turned out like that, for God's sake. What the hell went wrong?"

"Who knows? I guess poor old Stan just lost his cool. He told me the Thanets'd had a hell of a time in Ulster and he was under the additional strain of being a deserter, which he didn't like as much as he'd thought he would. I suppose the sight of Shwedi hacking at Anscudden with a butcher's knife was enough to push him over the edge. Jesus, I don't blame him: it wasn't pretty."

"It's the new-look Libyan justice. Or rather, it's medieval but recently revived."

I hadn't even taken off my coat. I now dropped it over a chair, found a match and lit the gas fire. It poppled and whined and threw out about as much heat as a Bunsen burner. Probably their South Sea Bubble gas or whatever it is.

"You shit," I said. "You knew I'd do things for you, so you used me."

"I'm sorry, Lee."

"That's good. You can be off now, then."

Selby shook his head. "I know how you must feel," he said. "It's understandable enough. I suppose in a way, it was rather flattering that we chose you like that. You were the one person reliable enough."

"Oh, Jesus," I said disgustedly.

"Look, Lee, I'll say I'm sorry just once more, but I had no choice at all; I was under pressure."

"I'm sure you were. Now go away."

"Severe pressure."

"From whom? Your bosses?"

"There've been one or two awkward deals they know about. Those M-16s that came through that South Vietnamese minister, for instance."

"Look, don't tell me your problems," I said. "Okay, you want me to believe the Agency's got a hold on you, or they're calling a loan, or something. I don't care. All I want is for you to get the hell out of here with your explanations and leave me in peace to earn a living doing what I like doing."

"That's a boring pose of naiveté, Lee," said Selby patiently. "You make your living by peddling firearms, and firearms are more than just pats of butter. They're political instruments. It's no good pretending to be a plain man caught in the middle of a bunch of double-crossing politicos. You know what the score is better than most."

Without looking at me, he put a hand in his coat pocket and produced a roll of money with an elastic band round it, which he tossed in my direction. I made no effort to catch it; it hit my chest and fell to the carpet with a heavy thud.

"Ten thousand," he said. "Just to demonstrate that I didn't come empty-handed."

"They never do," I said to nobody in particular. "Okay, what's the catch?"

"Javits."

"What about him?"

"He's become a nuisance."

I put down my glass abruptly and stood up. "Look," I said. "I've been pretty patient so far, all things considered, but all of a sudden I've had the whole thing. If Javits is a thorn in your organization's side, then good luck to him. He's the guy I work for, and without being the Corporation's slave, I'm pretty happy. Agreed, he's a strange character, even idiosyncratic. But I don't mind that, and I'm glad some people find him a nuisance."

"You're being emotional, Lee. You haven't got the information I have. I may as well tell you now that like it or not, you're in it up to here. I had no alternative to roping you in for the *Trebizond* business, nor do I have any choice now: I was told to. Believe me, I held out as long as I could, but it wasn't any good."

"Why should I believe you? Why me?"

"Because you're close to Javits. You work for him; he trusts you."

"But why the hell does the Agency want to get at Javits?" I asked. "What's he done to them? He went along with your plan all right."

"Sure," said Selby. "But it's not so much what he's done that worries people as what he's planning to do."

"And what's that?" I asked.

Selby nodded his head sorrowfully. "I can tell you that simply because you're already in too deep, Lee, even if you don't know it. It's not information you could ever use, because it would cost you your life."

"You terrify me."

"I shall, I promise. Your boss Javits has made a big mistake. He's let it be known that he has a good many files which he's been adding to over the years. Old Javits is getting on for sixty, you know, and he's been in the game for over thirty years. Most people think he started sometime after 1945, but in fact he began dealing in arms round about the outbreak of the Second World War, and he's been at it ever since. Of course, he's sold arms to both sides in a conflict: guys in your business have been doing that since Zaharoff ensured that the British got hell knocked out of them at the Dardanelles by British weapons. As you know, plenty of Allied soldiers in World War Two got little holes drilled through them by Allied bullets fired from Allied guns in the hands of the enemy in various places around the globe. Often it's turned out to have been Javits who sold them.

"You can say," went on Selby, "that it's only to be expected, because you arms merchants don't take sides: you merely supply a commodity to whoever has the money to buy it. That's certainly as good a way as any of sidestepping any hassle about moral issues and principles and suchlike. But that's not the point right now. The point is that Javits has obviously learned a lot about the various *Realpolitik* decisions taken by countries he's dealt with, most of which would be more than embarrassed if the news leaked out. In one case I can think of, even some quite old information could bring a present government down."

I leaned over and wrestled with the gas tap to see if I could coax some more heat out of the fire. "Shit," I said. "Everyone in the trade learns information about political decisions. They keep quiet because if they didn't, they'd lose out. Discretion is the better part of business, and it's more obviously desirable to be discreet in the weapons trade than in practically any other."

"Sure," said Selby, "everyone knows little secrets. But many of them come out later when some eager young journalist starts probing around trying to find out who supplied the arms to the rebels or which Great Power supported the loyalists. The people who get hottest under the collar about such revelations are mostly the middle-class liberals who read heavy Sunday papers. Everyone else is cynical enough to admit that it's slightly ironic when America can be shown to have sold arms to both sides somewhere, but it's nothing to make a song and dance about. It's axiomatic to the capitalist system that making money is an end in its own right, and people expect it to happen.

"Certainly Javits knows all the filth, but where he's specialized is in keeping files on the individuals he deals with. That's why your Corporation's been so successful—because each time someone calls on him to negotiate, he only has to look up his file, and ten to one the minister he's dealing with will turn out to be a guy he knew as a private citizen years ago in the dear dead days that have slipped everybody else's memory. So old Javits'll know exactly what pressures to apply if necessary. Nobody else in the trade's ever done this before, because on the face of it it's appallingly stupid and dangerous. But your man hasn't let that bother him."

"Christ," I said. "He must be out of his mind."

"Yes," admitted Selby, "as a matter of fact, we think he may be. You may not know, but he's just founded the ISPT —the International Society for Political Truth—with himself as President. In a few days' time, he's going to pledge himself publicly to bring out a monthly publication giving details of the lives and dealings of the world's political figures. A year's subscription will be extremely expensive, I've no doubt, but it'll be required reading for anyone interested in the way the world continues to be run by venal human beings rather than by the saints Javits apparently expects. Presumably he'll have special terms for anybody wishing to buy up an entire edition."

"I don't believe it," I said.

"Think, Lee," urged Selby impatiently. "What the hell do you imagine Javits wanted to ask Anscudden those questions for? That was a real giveaway, and it proved he's nuts because he made the mistake of mentioning it in front of me. He knew my connection with the Agency. That was a bad mistake for him to have made."

"Jesus," I said, "the whole thing's too improbable."

"It's a fact. I'm afraid the truth is sad and commonplace rather than sinister: he's going out of his mind. It happens to a lot of people. It's just unfortunate that it's happening to a man with a great deal of power but subject to none of the constitutional safeguards that enable men to get rid of mad kings, dotty Popes and insane presidents. A crazy arms salesman with a moral ax to grind hasn't cropped up before."

"No. But it's no problem. He can be uncropped, can't he? It's the sort of thing your lot specialize in."

Selby sighed. "That's more difficult than you'd suppose. None of the countries in which he has branches would like it to happen there, because they have mixed feelings about Javits. They partly like him, because he's well known, infinitely respectable and good for the economy; they partly fear for what he might know and for what he might leave behind if he were assassinated. Furthermore, Javits himself is well guarded and believes himself invulnerable."

"In this game, that's a sure sign of insanity," I admitted.

"Undoubtedly. So if anyone's going to do it, it'll have to be somebody who has no connections with any particular country or agency."

"I don't know whom you've got in mind," I said, "but I want it clear right now that none of this includes me. Not in any shape or form. I work for Javits, and I'm not helping to get him knocked off to suit you or the CIA."

"That's too bad, Lee," said Selby quietly, "because you're it."

I stared at him. "You must be joking," I said. "Why me? I'm just an arms dealer, not an assassin. The guys you want live down the Earls Court Road; they're tough and mad and desperate for money and adventure. You'll have no difficulty recognizing them: they've all got Belgian first names and

Irish surnames and speak with Rhodesian accents. Just find anybody called Raoul O'Hare drinking beer in Earls Court and he'll be your man."

"No good, Lee; it's got to be someone we know—someone efficient and reliable. But above all, it's got to be someone on the inside—actually in the Corporation. I'm sorry; that makes it you."

"Fuck off, Selby," I said. "You've pulled your last filthy trick on me for old time's sake. Now go and find yourself a tame hit man. I'm no bloody hired murderer."

"You killed aboard the *Trebizond*."

"Self-defense. Anyway, who'd know about that?"

"Captain Ratnayaka, to name one. Then there's Malta. Your part in that hasn't become generally known, has it? I wonder if anybody's thought to match up all the bullets with all the guns? It's funny how neatly dead everybody got. The Maltese police may not get all the practice that Scotland Yard has, but even they must have thought it odd that at least two people would need to have killed each other simultaneously."

"As a matter of fact, that's exactly what did happen."

"Was it? I think we could help out the Maltese police with a much more plausible story. Mind you, it'd be a pity. So far you've come out of this with a clean slate and rather a lot of our money."

"Jesus," I said.

"Also," went on Selby remorselessly, "there's always the question of your license to deal in firearms here. Few businesses that need to operate discreetly have no skeletons in their cupboards, and I don't suppose Lee & Savernake's any different. I expect something or other might be found to interest the Mets or the Home Office or even the Foreign

Office. Your trading days would be over. You might even do well not having to jump bail."

I was silent. "God, you shit," I said finally.

Selby nodded. "I am that," he agreed. "But I'm over a barrel too, don't forget. Still, somewhere in Javits' files will be your own dossier. If he's allowed to go ahead and publish, quite a lot might get out anyway."

"I'll think about it," I said.

"I'm afraid not; it's already been thought about for you. Your job now is to get your boss together with his files, copies of this bean-spilling journal and other relevant things, and dynamite the lot. I agree there aren't many places in Europe where you can blow people up without exciting comment, but the good thing about munitions stores is that they sometimes go up of their own accord."

"Where are these files of his?" I asked tiredly.

"That's what nobody knows for certain. They might be in Vienna or they might be in the heart of Midlothian. But they've got to be somewhere he can get at them quickly in order to write these journal things. My bet," said Selby, "is that you'll find them in Trieste."

I bent down and picked up the roll of dollars he had tossed at me. "The very worst thing about your information is that it's quite often right," I said.

"You'd better believe it," agreed Selby.

15

I flew down to Vienna the following day and made for Javits' flat off Königstrasse. The desk clerk in the hall looked at me as if he'd never seen me before, ran his eyes carefully over me, waved me to a ludicrous gold chair with a high back and embroidered seat and reached for his white telephone. After a soft exchange, he said, "You may go upstairs please, Herr Mag . . . Herr Mig . . ."

"McGundrell," I said shortly. He didn't smile apologetically. I took the lift and went up to the penthouse. I emerged into the black-and-white decor and was met by Frick, who frisked me as expertly as ever. Not even old Stan could have taught him anything. Then he showed me into the front room with the double glazing and left me alone in the middle of acres of black carpet dotted here and there with clumps of white furniture and a white poodle asleep in front of the fire. Next to the fire was a vast copper bucket full of fir cones. I thought of the film I'd seen in Hamburg and was just wondering where these had been when Javits came in very quietly and said, "Ah, Lee. Nice to see you again. Had yourself a good rest?"

"So-so," I told him. It was only now that I fully realized

the man's obsession with the contrast of black and white. On the previous visit, he'd been wearing gray slacks and a colored shirt. Now, however, it was as if the informality had been replaced by a manic sort of high seriousness. He was dressed in a very severe black suit, a starched white shirt and a coal-black tie. He looked like a professional mourner—but only if you can imagine a professional mourner with pink eyes, colorless skin spotted with pigment and crisp gingerish hair.

"Drink?" he asked me.

"Too early," I said. "I'd like a coffee, though."

He rang a bell, and the girl who'd served us before appeared with her trolley. She had also undergone a sartorial change. The dirndl skirt in bright peasant colors had gone, to be replaced by a plain black dress with long white gloves. It looked most peculiar—rather as if she'd not yet had time to change after going to the opera or some other classy pursuit the night before.

"Look, Lee," said Javits when she had left, "I've got a problem here I think you can handle. But before anything else, let me give you this," and he handed me the envelope containing Stanno's money. "That's my part of the bargain, right?"

"Thanks."

"Uh, I'm sorry to have to say this, Lee, but I guess I've decided to wind up the Corporation. I know, I know—that means you'll be out of a job. But before it comes to that, you've plenty of earning opportunity left. You remember Teich, my chief armorer in Italy? Well, he's gone sick and I've got a big job to do."

"Like making an inventory?"

"Right, Lee. I wish it didn't have to be this way, but I'm getting old. I've been in this business too long, and I'm tired of it. I'm sick of the lies and double-dealing and corruption, so I'm selling out and getting out."

"It's taken you a good many years to decide it's too nasty to stay in," I said sourly.

Javits sighed and shook his orange-and-white head. "You can't needle me, Lee. I'm no bleeding-heart all of a sudden. But I've had an ulterior motive."

"Like making money?"

"Making money came into it, sure, but only for my Foundation."

"Foundation?"

"Maybe you haven't yet heard of it, Lee, but you will. The International Society for Political Truth is going to upset a lot of people, believe me; a whole lot of people. Yessir."

"What is it?" I asked.

He shook his head. "It'd spoil it if I gave too many secrets away. But in a week's time you'll know, and so will a lot of other people around the world. That's the day the first number of my monthly journals will be published. They'll be known as the *Vulcan Bulletins*. Don't you think that's a good name? For instance, what does the word 'Vulcan' mean to you, apart from some mythological crap?"

"It's the name of an obsolete British bomber," I said.

"Goddam it, I keep telling you that you won't needle me, so why do you bother to try? A Vulcan, as you damn well know, is the M-61 cannon. And what do you know about that?"

"It's a Grade-A nasty weapon," I said. "It's General Electric's version of their Minigun, which itself is a sort of wild derivation from the old Gatling. Whereas the Gatlings had six barrels cranked mechanically by hand, the Minigun is fired electrically. It fires seven-point-six-two-millimeter rounds at a rate of six thousand per minute. The Vulcan's much the same, only worse, because it fires a twenty-mil round. I believe somebody made efforts to get it banned from all combat except for ground-to-air use, because it was supposed to be too appalling for use against personnel."

"Check," said Javits, "although Christ alone knows what they think flies an aircraft. Monkeys, maybe. But that's the Vulcan. So I'm calling my monthlies the *Vulcan Bulletins,* and I'm sure as hell using them against personnel. I love that title, Lee. Do you know who gave it to me?"

"No," I said.

"My mother."

"Your mother?"

"That's right, my old mom. And let me tell you right away, Lee, that this is one goddam topic you don't laugh at. To me it's sacred. That old lady's the most wonderful person I know, and she's given me the most important responsibility I've ever had."

A certain gleam had come into Javits' eyes, but whether of tears or of downright madness it wasn't easy to tell. I found myself avoiding having to look directly at him, and I stared instead at the poodle in front of the fire and thought what a horrible little pink anus it had.

"My mom," Javits was saying, "has left me with a sacred duty, an obligation. She's speechless, you know, Lee. Such is the cruelty of our earthly circumstance that she's been without the power of speech for ten years. But her brain still has all its old agility; I know that because I can see her eyes move when I visit her. She's in the best damn nursing home that money can buy," he added proudly, "in Peoria, Illinois. You wouldn't believe what I pay monthly. I nearly have a stroke myself when I pick up the tab at the end of the year. But what's money?" Javits spread out his hands in a rhetorical gesture. The same blotches of pigment covered his palms as well.

"I think you understand, Lee," he said. "I can say these things without you getting cheap laughs."

"Oh, yes," I assured him. The poodle's arse winked at me as the dog tensed its muscles and stretched. To be frank, I no longer knew how to react to this amazing confession.

"If I thought you were laughing," he added, rather spoiling the portrait of sensitive intimacy he was painting, "I'd get mad enough to maybe shoot you."

"Why should I laugh?" I wanted to know. Why indeed? It was more chilling than funny.

"Hell, I don't know," said Javits. "Folks are odd. There're a lotta people who think it's somehow funny an arms dealer having a mother. So anyway, I used to visit her a lot at first when I mostly lived in the States. I got to sitting by her bed and telling her what I was doing and what was happening in the world. And I knew she was interested from the way she rolled her eyes; she'd always been pretty clued up about politics. Suddenly, Lee"—he leaned towards me—"suddenly I knew she was talking right back to me. She wasn't actually speaking the words, of course, because of the paralysis. But I knew what she was saying, all the same. I know my mom like the back of my hand." He laid a thick white forefinger on the gravemarked back of his left hand.

"What she was saying was that she was proud of me, that

I was a damn good businessman. She was saying that I was the only clean guy in a dirty line of business and that I had a duty to remain in the trade as an example, I guess, of how it's possible to be *ethical* even in armaments."

I nodded blankly and put down my coffee cup on the floor.

"You want some more coffee?" he asked.

"Well, I was just thinking that perhaps it's time for a drink," I said. "It's a little later than it was."

"Sure." He reached out and pressed the bell again. The girl in the long black dress and the white gloves came in with her trolley and took our cups. "Fix Mr. McGundrell a Scotch, Heidi. I'll have one too."

"Is she really called Heidi?" I asked when the girl had left.

"Sure is. Why not?" He took a gulp of his whisky. "Where was I? Oh, yeah. My old mom pointing out how ethical I was. Well, hell, with a mom like that, how could I be otherwise? I was fed on ethics as a kid, and you can bet that she could be pretty fierce if I started acting up or was up to no good. Yessir, she'd send me to bed with my little ass in flames."

I stared at the whisky I held, trying to suppress the urge to visualize this bizarre image, not wanting to know if the gravemarks extended to areas now covered by the severe suit and dazzling shirt.

"But it was worth it, Lee, because I learned manners and I learned how to behave in a civilized fashion. She took good care of that, bless her heart. And now there isn't anything I wouldn't do for her."

"What's this sacred commitment she gave you?" I inquired at length.

Javits stood up with a visionary gleam in his eye; there was no mistaking it this time as he straddled the white rug in front of the hearth, his glass in his left hand, his right making sideways chopping motions as if at the necks of invisible opponents.

" 'Go out,' she told me. 'Go out and show the world its own face.' Go out and let everybody know that behind the Presidential speeches, the United Nations resolutions, the messages of peace and the pledges of goodwill are filthy, corrupt men, Lee; wheelers and dealers, lying and miming and cutting each other's throats for the sake of a bit of power or a few million lousy bucks. That's what she told me, and by golly, it's all true. It's taken me practically twenty years to discover all the depths to which the human animal will sink, but that sweet little innocent old lady kind of knew it all along. It's almost like a special genius, that sort of wisdom, I guess. Well, now I know it too, and the time has come for me to make my knowledge public.

"I'm selling out, Lee; I'm quitting. It's all been a means to an end, to do what Mama wants—*wanted* me to do. I've begun afresh from the moment Mom . . ." he choked, and I looked up to see the pinkish eyes bright with tears. He turned away and stared at the traffic down below, crawling along inaudibly in the Viennese lunch-hour jam. "She passed away ten days ago," he said, and I could hardly hear his voice.

"I'm very sorry," I said. I sounded about as convincing as Selby had.

"No, why should you be? You never met her. But the loss was yours, I promise you. A very wonderful old lady . . . perhaps *the* most wonderful old lady that ever lived. I gave her the sort of send-off that only a son could give.

163

I've been out of town because I was over there in Peoria, Illinois, showing her how much she was loved. Fifty thousand dollars that funeral cost, Lee, and it wasn't a cent too much. I only hope you can do the same for your mama. Have you got a mama?"

I thought of my old mum as I saw her last, a few months previously, slopping round the house in Jubilee Terrace wearing slippers and swearing like a trooper. She too was full of warmth, but only when she was also full of Guinness; and she knew no more about world politics than the budgerigars she prodded gently with a blunt wooden knitting needle to make them twitter.

"Yes, I've got a mother."

"You're a lucky man, Lee." He turned back from the window and sketched in the air with his free hand. "Six black horses, their hoofs all painted black too, pulling a gun carriage smack through the middle of Peoria, Illinois, on a Wednesday morning. And on the gun carriage lay Mama in the whitest coffin you ever saw. Snow Enamel, it was called—all hand-rubbed. Cost a bomb, you believe me. Slowly, slowly, all the way up, and the traffic all at a standstill and just a few ugly mothers blowing their goddam horns, all the way up to the First Reformed Church of Zion. And I looked at Mama's face during that service, Lee, all serene and beautiful, watching me out of the top half of that Snow Enamel coffin, and I'm not ashamed to admit it, I cried. I cried like a little boy. But although she'd passed over, I could still hear her telling me that she didn't want expensive memorials and plinths and urns and vases and all that—although, of course, she got 'em. What she wanted was for me to be her memorial; and by golly, I knew I was, right from that moment on.

"Since then, I've stopped all business dealing here, except stuff that was already in the pipeline. We had certain commitments we had to honor."

"Such as the *Trebizond* deal," I said.

"Right. And it looks like I might have something going with a bunch of kids down in Africa or someplace. But apart from that, I'm through. Now, like I said, what with Teich going sick, I'd like for you to help check the inventory of the stuff we've got in stock. We'll start with the main store in Trieste, but we'll get around to your British end in time. I mean to wind up this Corporation in a neat and businesslike fashion. The more money I can sell out for, the more I'll have to spend on the *Bulletins*.

"Now, you'll find everything's listed, of course, but only by batches like in London. As you know, a lot of those batches were bought under an averaging system, so there's quite a few shitty guns mixed up. I want you to go through them and weed out the ones you think should be junked. We might also have a category of arms that need some benchwork done on them, but not too much. Reckon you can handle that?"

"Sure," I said. "But it makes you wonder if averaging pays off."

"Hell, it brings the import duties way down. I'll give you an example. When you start in, you'll find twenty-five thousand Iranian Model 1930 rifles. You know the ones?"

"Vaguely. I seem to remember they're seven-point-nine-two-millimeter jobs based on the Czech ZB ninety-eight/ twenty-nine—the old Mauser design. It's the short rifle, isn't it?"

"Correct," said Javits, with a certain surprise. "You certainly know your small arms, Lee, like I've always said.

Well, there're quite a few useless rifles in that batch. They brought down the average value on which we had to pay duty. Actually, you'll find a hell of a lot in mint condition. The Iranians unloaded them when they started replacing them by M-Ones for their Army."

"I can do it, but it'll take a bit of time."

"I want it done as fast as possible."

"Sure. But there's a limit to how fast anybody can inspect twenty-five thousand rifles. And there's a lot of other stuff, too. Do you want batches of ammunition sorted as well?"

"Could do. There's still some prewar boxes knocking around. You'd better check it out. I reckon to dump everything you reject, Lee. I've got faith in you. We'll take whatever you don't like, load it up and dump it in the ocean. When I come to auction off my stuff, I want it all to be usable. No crap, you understand? No deadweight iron you can't even cannibalize for spares. A clean sweep."

"I reckon it can be done. What are you paying?"

"Say five hundred a month bonus?"

"Sounds good."

"It is." Javits smiled, and those startlingly perfect teeth came into view. "You know, Lee, you've always impressed the hell out of me with that knowledge of yours. Sure, it's your job and all, but I can't remember a single time when you've gotten a weapon wrong. I'd give something just to see you baffled for once. So, just for the hell of it, what do you make of these?" He reached into his desk drawer and fished out a couple of handguns.

The first was clearly new, and I thought at first it was the French MAB pistol. Then I took a closer look at it as it lay in Javits' hand, unfortunately with the manufacturer's name downwards. Still, I had a pretty good idea, and I even seemed to remember having fired one.

"German," I said. "It's Heckler and Koch's model VP-seventy."

"Very good," said Javits. "Can you tell me anything else about it?"

"Yes, I think there's something unusual about the action. Oh, yes—the hammer isn't cocked automatically after firing a shot. It ejects and reloads, but you have to release the trigger and pull it again to fire another. It's got a pretty weighty double action, too, so it's not likely to go off accidentally. You can carry the thing with a round chambered, giving you nineteen shots, which is pretty good. Nine-mil. Parabellum, of course."

"And what's this for?" Javits pointed a white finger at a slot in the rear of the receiver.

"Oh, yes, I remember that; a very nice piece of design," I said. "H and K provide a detachable stock which you can fit to the pistol to give you full-automatic fire. The stock also doubles as a holster, incidentally. There's a lug on the front of the stock that fits into this slot on the gun itself and alters the operating system to full-auto. You can only fire the pistol on full-auto when the stock's fitted. The cyclic rate's way up around two thousand rounds per minute, so on the stock there's a selector switch that you can turn to get bursts of only three rounds at a time before you have to release the trigger and fire again. Very neat, that."

"You amaze me," said Javits. "Now how about this one?"

The second pistol looked, if not out of the Ark, then possibly home-made. It was very short, obviously single-shot and made like a child's toy from ordinary thin metal stamping. It was unpainted and unblued. There were no identification figures on it; it was sterile.

"May I?" I took it from him.

"Sure; go ahead. Ever seen one before?"

"No." I shook my head. I looked at the muzzle. "Forty-five?"

"Yup."

The trigger guard curved upwards over the end of the stubby barrel, where it petered out in a sort of rudimentary foresight. "One of those cheap disposable jobs for special service," I hazarded.

"That's right—that's just what it is," said Javits. "American-made for the OSS during World War Two. The OSS used to pass them on to various underground movements. They're all stampings and regular tubing with a couple of screws thrown in. The barrel isn't rifled, as you no doubt noticed. Dead cheap to produce, and pretty effective, too." He opened a small compartment in the butt. "You could carry a few extra rounds in here," he said, "but it's very much a single-shot job. Hell, there isn't even an extractor: you've got to push out the empty case with a goddam stick. I got this out in the Pacific; it's like a souvenir. They were damned effective against the Japs, you know. If a guy knows he's only got one shot, he sure as hell makes certain where it goes. Old Wild Bill Donovan himself was pretty keen on these little guns. You know, General Donovan. He was the head of the OSS at the time. He reckoned they were ideal for dropping to sympathetic natives. There was an instruction sheet enclosed with each pistol; no words, just simple pictures. That's a good weapon."

Javits wrapped it up in a cloth and stowed it back in the drawer. "The VP's for you," he said, handing the other gun to me.

"You're kidding," I said.

"Hell no, Lee. I had a little bet on with myself, and I've just lost. Believe me, you've earned it; you know a lot more about the damn thing than I do."

"Thanks very much."

"Aw, shit. Okay now, when do you want to start? All that stuff from Malta's back at Trieste. In fact, I left that warehouse a whole lot emptier than you did."

"Hit the headlines, didn't it?"

"That was something, I'm telling you, Lee. The place really hummed for a day or two. But we kept it under wraps, like I said."

"I hope it stays there," I said. I checked that the pistol was unloaded and tucked it into the waistband of my trousers. "There's only one thing that puzzles me," I said.

"What's that?"

"Well, this journal of yours, the ISPT thing . . ."

"The *Vulcan Bulletin.*"

"Yes. Won't you be treading on a hell of a lot of toes?"

A look of determination tinged with self-satisfaction came onto Javits' face.

"Sure I will. Not just toes, either, you can bet. Nuts and faces, too."

"Aren't you afraid somebody'll try to knock you off?"

"No," said Javits. "I wouldn't be surprised if they try, but they won't succeed."

"How the hell can you be so sure?" I asked.

"Are you psychic?" The pinkish eyes rolled towards me.

"I don't mean do you believe in the occult necessarily, but what about the stars? Are you interested in astrology, Lee?"

It was my turn to be emphatic. "No," I said.

"I'm surprised at you, I really am. You know, you've led a dangerous life; you've seen killing and all sorts of nasty things. But you've never been badly hurt, have you?"

"Not yet, maybe."

"There, I knew I was right. Well, did you ever stop to ask yourself how that was? Did you think you were just lucky? That you had all the breaks?"

"Not necessarily. Luck's the name they give for trajectories' obeying rigid physical laws that make it impossible for the bullet to hit you."

"Very scientific," said Javits. "Very arrogant, too, if I may say so. Up until now, you've been protected by the conjunctions of your stars."

"I have?"

"Certainly. And so have I. I have complete faith, Lee. What's more, my mom was psychic too, and she could see my life ahead of me when I was a baby. 'My son will live to be a hundred,' she used to say, and I know she was right."

"Don't all mothers say that?" I asked.

"Perhaps some do. But my mom never told an untruth in her life. She had Knowledge, you know." He spelled it with a capital. "If she said I will live to be a hundred, then a hundred is what I'll live to be. Oh, yes, they'll try to kill me. But they won't succeed. They'll have to come through Frick first, and believe me, that boy's loyal unto death, as they say."

"He's good," I admitted.

"Sure is. One of the best. Hell no, I'm not scared. Now,

I guess that's business settled. What say we go out and grab a bite to eat?"

We picked up Frick as we got into the lift. Or rather, he picked us up, in a way that gave the impression that he had practically been inside the room with us. Suddenly, unobtrusively, he was there. We went down together, not speaking. At the bottom, Javits waved a white hand at the clerk behind his mahogany desk.

"Out to lunch," he said. "Back about three."

"Very good, Herr Javits," said the faithful fellow.

We came down the shallow marble steps onto the pavement and crossed to the curb to pick up a cab. It really wasn't such a bad place to live, I reflected, provided you had enough sound insulation to blot out the traffic roar that was now sweeping over us like a tide. There was even a species of tree growing in the pavement, one of a series of half a dozen which were staggered at intervals of fifty yards or so on alternate sides of the street. With them, at least, you could get some idea of what time of year it was just by glancing out your penthouse window. It would be about the only way.

We were right in our assessment of Frick. He had grabbed Javits and shoved him behind the tree practically before the big Mercedes saloon had got its nearside front wheel onto the edge of the pavement. The driver gunned the engine, and the bumper scythed past my shins and slammed glancingly into the trunk with a great bang of dented metal. Dead twigs and a few shriveled leaves rained down onto our heads as the Mercedes bounced back into the road, still accelerating, its right wing crumpled by the sideswipe. Javits was just behind the tree, and Frick had now let go of his coat. Instead, he had gone into a professional shooter's crouch, holding his gun two-handedly on the retreating car. Javits knocked the gun aside with his forearm.

"Not here, Frick," he said. "Not in broad goddam daylight."

Frick looked angry, even hurt, and put the gun back in his open-fronted shoulder holster. It had all happened so fast that few people would have seen the gun, although the noise of the impact and the careening Mercedes had got them interested enough to begin to tear their eyes away from the pavement a couple of yards in front of their own feet. Javits looked calmer than Frick, although his severe black jacket had been torn by Frick's sudden grip and a seam gaped whitely on the back. The desk clerk came down the steps of the entrance in one leap, his hand reaching inside his own jacket.

"Cool it, everyone," said Javits, shrugging the bunched cloth of his jacket back into shape and brushing the leaves and twigs off his orange hair. He turned to me. My shins felt cold, as if from the wind of the bumper, and I was still trying to memorize the number. "There, Lee, what did I tell you? They can try, but they won't succeed."

"Thanks to Frick, here," I said.

"Sure, Frick's included in my stars too. Did you see the driver?"

I shook my head. "Tinted windows," I said. "But I got the number."

"Forget it. It was stolen anyway."

Curious people had now begun to stop and stare. Two small boys were examining the ragged white wound in the tree trunk and were giving each other yet more lurid accounts of the incident—which, probably, neither had seen. Javits decided to go back in and change his jacket. As I turned to follow, I saw a dumpy figure over on the other side of the road. I felt certain I should recognize it, but before my brain had made the right connections it was lost among the passersby.

16

We flew down to Trieste in Javits' Lear jet, landing at Monfalcone and driving the last twenty or so miles down the coast road. The sea was flat calm and looked like gray cardboard, on which a couple of ships heading for Trieste showed up starkly, leaving black smudges of smoke rising undisturbed beneath the high cloud base. It's a curious place—remaining Italian in the last analysis, but only just. It ought to be in Yugoslavia, but the border, instead of cutting into the sea at the top of the Gulf, bends at the last moment to permit a narrow strip of Italian soil to creep a few miles round the corner like a territorial appendix. At the end of the appendix is Trieste, the border finally curling round it within a few kilometers. The town itself is built up against the hills that curve around the Bay of Muggia, and from it the three major roads climb up to the striped barriers and flagpoles on the frontier.

"Quite a useful place," observed Javits as we drove into town. "Like in Vienna, you've got rail access to Eastern Europe, but here you've got a port as well. It's a bit of a roundabout damn journey by train; the stuff usually comes via Prague, Budapest, Zagreb and Ljubljana, but at least it gets here. All you have to do is load it on a ship and you're away."

There was a Javits Corporation office in the city center, but we drove straight to the warehouse, and I was once more aware of how much money and ingenuity Javits had expended on his facilities. On the south side of Trieste was the tiny Bay of Muggia. The apex of this bay was a basin which was constructed to supplement the main port to the north. Few commercial vessels used it, apparently, as it was empty except for a handful of fishing smacks which presumably belonged to the hamlet of Aquilinia, on the opposite shore. At the neck of the basin was a low, rounded hill perhaps three hundred feet high with a small road running round the bottom. We drove round it, watched by a few slum-dwellers from the windows of their desperate houses, until we came to two warehouses much like the one on Malta, standing side by side with their far ends wedged up against the hill. A single track of railway lines led from a junction in front of them down across the road and onto a wharf on the other side. Above the great hangar doors of the warehouses was a large signboard which bore the name EDERA S.A. It had often puzzled me.

"Edera?" I asked.

"It's Italian for 'ivy,'" said Javits proudly. "My mom's name is Ivy. Was," he corrected himself.

The car drew up on the concrete apron in front, and we all got out. Frick rang a bell by a small door marked *Informazione,* which opened almost at once. A young man I'd not met before with a black tie and one hand nonchalantly inside his jacket relaxed and smiled when he caught sight of Javits.

"Good morning, sir," he said, and he stood aside to let us in.

"Morning, Guido; meet Mr. McGundrell, here. Lee's going to be working with us for a while on the inventory. *Inventario,* you know?"

We'd come into an office, full of files and telephone directories and old invoices with coffee rings on them. I doubted that they had much to do with the Corporation's business; he would be better at set design than at homely squalor. A metal side door led into the adjacent warehouse, and we went in, Guido switching on the powerful overhead lights as we did. The place was piled high with crates and boxes, with narrow alleys leading off between them, dividing them into carefully organized lots. I saw that a pair of railway lines came in under the main doors and extended the length of the warehouse.

"Mostly transit stuff, this," said Javits, waving a hand. We went through a door that linked both warehouses together. The other one was practically full of Ferret scout cars. "Also transit," he said. "You don't have to worry about any of it."

"Where are these going?" I asked.

"Tanzania," said Javits. "They decided they could do with some transportation as well. I happened to hear that one of those places in Saudi Arabia or somewhere was trying to unload Ferrets—where was it, Guido?"

"One of the Oman states, you said, sir. Dhofar, I believe you say."

"Hell, somewhere like that . . . Anyway, they wanted to re-equip with APCs only. I suppose in country like that there isn't much point in scouting unless you have some troops with you as a backup. If you run into trouble, an

176

armored personnel carrier's a lot more use than a Ferret. So I asked Tanzania if they wanted some scout cars, and they said yes, by golly, they could use fifty of those, so here they are. I'll have to get them resprayed."

The Ferrets were painted for desert use—sand-colored, with Arabic inscriptions on them in white paint. Command vehicles had flag colors painted on the front and back next to the number, but as I had no idea what the Omani national flag looked like, I couldn't identify it. Javits led the way down the central aisle between them, stopping now and then to point out a tire with a chunk of rubber knocked out of its shoulder or a pool of oil underneath a vehicle's sump.

"They'll like 'em," he said. "Couple of repairs here and there and a new paint job. They can go roaring round Tanzania to their hearts' content." It seemed he looked upon his clients as a bunch of joyriders.

We reached the end of the warehouse. Guido opened a panel in the wall, which disclosed two keyholes and an illuminated button. He produced a key on a light chain from his pocket. Javits searched his jacket and finally brought out a key of his own. I wondered why he didn't keep it on a chain like Guido's out of sheer convenience. They inserted them and turned them simultaneously, Javits pressing the button as they did so. Immediately, a siren climbed to a howl somewhere in the warehouse and a large pair of double doors drew aside. We stepped through into the wide passageway beyond; a relay clicked and the doors shut again behind us with a low rumble. The noise of the siren could be heard falling in the distance. There was another panel with keyholes on this side of the door too, and I noticed Javits stuck his key in and left it there, doubtless

177

to save himself the trouble of searching for it when he came to go out. Guido looked as though he disapproved of this sort of laxity, but perhaps he always looked like that. The corridor was painted white and was about twenty yards long. The walls were alive with crimson slogans which said, POSITIVELY NO SMOKING BEYOND THIS POINT. YOU HAVE BEEN WARNED.

"Not really necessary," said Javits as he saw me eyeing them. "We do have a few demolition charges and suchlike up in the munitions room, but all this is quite safe."

"All this" was one of the largest enclosed spaces I had ever been in. It had been hollowed out of the center of the hill and lined with gray concrete, rows of thick pillars supporting the roof, in which high-wattage lights were sunk behind grilles. It was like one of the vast underground car parks such as the one near London's Marble Arch beneath Park Lane and Hyde Park, only a lot higher. The entire space seemed occupied by gun racks which stretched into the distance. Avenues wide enough to permit maneuvering by forklift trucks led off between the racks. They were about thirty feet apart, and each had a letter of the alphabet above it on a square white sign. Running across the hall was a subsidiary grid of narrow lanes, which were numbered. Hence, any particular block or lot of weapons could be identified immediately.

"Jesus," I said, "it's going to take bloody months to sort through this lot."

"Nope," said Javits decisively. "Sure, there's a whole heap of stuff here, but most of it's okay. There's just a few lots I bought under averaging. Where were those Persian rifles, Guido?"

"C-seven, sir."

"Right." We found C7 and there they began, because twenty-five thousand rifles cover a hell of a lot of space, even when closely racked in tiers. That's getting on for a hundred tons of weapons.

"At a glance, some of them don't look too bad," I said. "I see you've got some different models mixed up."

"I have?" queried Javits. "They all look like 1930s to me."

"No, you've got some 1949s among them," I said, reaching one down. "It's an identical weapon except that the bands and sling swivels are different. It makes no odds."

"This boy knows everything, I'm telling you," Javits said to Guido. Guido eyed me sourly. I turned the flange of the safety catch upwards so that it pointed between Safe and Fire, eased the bolt stop aside and removed the weapon's bolt. A quick turn to the left and the firing pin and cocking piece could be withdrawn.

"Take a look at the pin," I said.

"Corrosion," said Javits.

"Right. All round the shoulder. Where it usually is." I put the bolt together again, replaced it, put the safety back on and racked the gun. "Do you count that?"

"No," said Javits. "Jesus, a bit of corrosion like that: what do you expect? That gun's over twenty years old. Only chuck 'em out if they're dangerous. We've got some old Czech twenty-fours you can cannibalize if you want. They use the same bolt. How many we got of those, Guido?"

"Only about sixty, sir. They're up on B-three."

"Well, use what you need, Lee. Guido, here, will tell you anything you want to know about our stock."

"Thanks. Do you mind if I wander around a bit on my own? I'd like to get familiar with the layout and see what you've got."

"Sure," said Javits with a wave, "help yourself. With that project I was telling you about, I've got work to do, so I'll let you get on. Say, Guido, tell me about final delivery arrangements for those Ferrets . . ." and he walked off with Guido in attendance. I made a mental note that the young man in the black tie needed watching and began wandering around.

It's quite impossible to explain the thrill I get out of arms stores. The first time I ever went inside one was when I was shown round the Buffs' armory at their Canterbury barracks as a kid. I'd been mesmerized then by the sight and smell of the weapons. The neatness of racked guns is gratifying to the eye: the uniform golden brown of the stocks, the same dull gleam off the matte metal parts—the sling and fore-end bands, the corners of the magazines, the edges of the bolts. Armories are quiet places, too. Except for the occasional tramp of boots down the concrete aisles, there is total silence, with perhaps just the faint rattle of a fan heater somewhere as it wafts the warm scents of metal polish and solvent and heavy oil about. Behind it all there is also the bright, bitter smell of brass and copper tarnishing imperceptibly, which is the smell inside ammunition boxes, together with that of the khaki paint they cover the cases with. The slings give off a smell of their own too, of webbing and old blanco, as do the thin fabric bandoliers in which .303 ammunition comes packed in clips of five. Those, at least, were the impressions indelibly left on me as a kid.

Since then, of course, armories have changed their smell slightly. Less blanco, different kinds of oil; but you still get the old familiar wafts from weapons of the previous period. For a long time they covered all military stuff in storage

180

with Cosmoline, which was a very efficient preservative, but sheer bloody murder to get off. It meant that weapons which had been treated were out of action until the Cosmoline had been removed. They don't use it any more now because it was so inconvenient, but you can still smell it around wherever you've got unused arms stored, especially World War II surplus. In the States nowadays they've taken to coating weapons all over in Teflon, which is fine except that it doesn't smell so good.

I moved down the avenues and across the lanes, occasionally taking down weapons and examining them. As far as I could see, Javits had been right: there was very little inferior stuff there, and anyway, he had good stores of spare parts. There were ten thousand spare Bren barrels, complete with carrying handles; there were also, for some reason, fifteen thousand bayonets in new leather sheaths to fit the Finnish M-62 assault rifle. I couldn't see any M-62s, but Javits had collected some Soviet AK-47s, of which the Finnish weapon is a modified version. However, I remembered that the bayonet fittings are different, so that the bayonets were not interchangeable.

I eventually came on the stores from which equipment had been drawn for our assault on the *Trebizond*: neatly packed USAF rubber dinghies dusty with French chalk and a rack of twenty-four High Standard Model 10 riot guns: the single empty slot had no doubt held the weapon I had mistakenly left aboard the ship at Malta. I wondered vaguely what Captain Demirel had done with it.

Grenades, mortar shells, bazooka rounds, antitank rockets, wire-guided missiles, small aerial incendiaries, parachute flares; altogether, many millions of dollars' worth of tidily racked and classified ordnance, which Javits was about to sell off—all because his mother had died and left him with a sacred pledge. It seemed impossible that such a veteran in a line of business not designed for the softhearted should be betrayed by a crippling attack of sentimentality. Nevertheless, I'd noted similar traits before in other supposedly hard men. It often seemed that the tougher they liked to appear, the more certain it was that they'd have some undignified weakness for their mothers, or animals, or vintage Hollywood musicals, or churchgoing. The really callous ones were invariably religious, I'd noticed.

"Most impressive," I said to Javits when we met up again. "You've got a lot of good hardware here."

"Sure do," he agreed. "But it's all gotta go, it's all gotta go."

"What's behind that heavy metal door up on the left?" I inquired. "The gray one?"

"That's just paper work in there: files and accounts, all that sort of thing. Archives." He didn't seem as if he was going to be any more forthcoming than that. I wondered if it was in that heavily locked room that the *Vulcan Bulletins* would be hatched each month.

Javits and Guido let us out of the store in the same way: with two keys. As we went through the doorway, I tried to see how the siren was wired up. There was a contact breaker in the frame and also, I noticed for the first time, another one behind it. Security was a lot better than it had been at Malta, but still a long way from impregnable. I caught Guido looking at me thoughtfully and decided that I'd shown enough interest for one day.

"I've got a new apartment in back of the city, out Villa Opicina way," said Javits, handing me a card with an address on it. "Anytime you want me outside work hours, just call me up as usual."

I found a hotel called the Sesana and got my feet up as quickly as possible. I must have dropped off pretty soon, and I awoke feeling a bit less jaded. I don't like all this moving around, and I seemed to have done nothing but travel over the last few days. By now it was dark, so I took myself out on one of those dreary quests for an evening meal.

However handy Trieste might have been for the armaments trade, it was pretty deficient in night life. That's the trouble with most border towns: they deal with people passing through, most of whom never spend the night. It was now November and the tourist season had long since finished, and apart from some of the local lads burning up and down the side streets on their motor scooters, the place was quiet. I found a restaurant near the port that served seafood and ordered something or other.

"*Pivo?*" inquired the waiter. Perhaps he thought I looked Yugoslavian.

"*Che?*"

"*Birra?*" the man corrected himself. I added a bottle of beer to the order and opened Irving Stone again for another go. It was altogether a miserable meal, and I would have liked to talk to somebody just to take my mind off squid and Michelangelo. But I wasn't feeling so damned sociable that I wanted to be followed half an hour later, which was what happened after I left the restaurant. I only got the merest glimpse when I glanced back, because whoever it was disappeared into a doorway. I found a small cobbled alley full of twilight and mangy cats rummaging through garbage at the side, tucked myself round the corner and waited. Sure enough; the rapid footsteps of somebody anxious not to be left behind, slowing as they approached the corner in case there was something unexpected around it. There was, but his caution didn't help him any as I reached out and grabbed the front of his coat with my left hand, getting in a good low blow with the stiffened fingers of my right. He folded abruptly with a retching noise and then rolled himself into a soundless ball at my feet. I bent over him.

"God Almighty," I said. "*Moleman.* I'm sorry, Mole."

When he had recovered sufficiently, I leaned him gently up against the wall.

"Christ," he gasped, opening his swimming eyes, "that was a nasty one."

"I'm terribly sorry, Mole," I said again. "How in hell could I have known it'd be you, of all people? I thought it was John Q. Citizen about to beat up on me." Suddenly a synapse clicked somewhere inside my brain. "You weren't in Vienna yesterday morning, were you?"

"Yes. I thought you'd been knocked off and I'd got there too late."

"It was Javits they were after, not me. But what were you doing there? Or here, come to that? Why aren't you in London?"

"I'm supposed to be your ally on the ground."

"Well," I said, surprised, "it's very kind of you, Mole. But I don't need one."

"Your friend Selby said you did. He said you'd need a cracksman."

I helped him to his feet. "Let's go and have a drink and you can tell me," I said. "Are you okay?"

Moleman stood there wincing. "I shan't bloody know, shall I? Not until I've tried it out."

We found a bar on the waterfront and sat ourselves at a tin table with Campari ashtrays let into the top.

"Anything you like, Mole. I really owe you this one."

He sniffed. "I'll have a beer," he said. "It's about the only thing you can trust."

"*Pivo*," I told the waiter.

"*Sì, Signore.*"

"Not bad," said Moleman when it arrived. "Usually you can't trust this foreign stuff."

I grinned. "You don't like being abroad?"

"No," he said shortly. "I can't understand what they say, and I can't eat what they bring. Otherwise, it's a ball of fun."

"So why did you come?"

"Like I told you, Selby insisted you'd need help but that you'd never have asked me in a million years."

"That's right," I told him seriously, "I wouldn't. I don't want you mixed up in a mess like this, Mole; it's not your line of country. It's not even mine. Don't worry, we'll get you on a flight tomorrow."

"Now, hang on, Lee. I never said I'd agree to go home, did I?"

I sighed. "How much do you know?"

"Not a lot. Selby said you had a job on that'd need a safe-man sooner or later. He said you'd never find anyone else quick enough who you could trust. He didn't say what was in the safe, but I gather it's on the confidential side."

"Damn right," I told him. "But there's no reason for you to know what it is, Mole. This whole business stinks, and the less you wind up knowing the better. But I'm sorry, you can't stay and that's final."

185

Moleman leaned forward, wincing as he did so. "Tough shit," he said; "I'm staying. If you need someone to open a safe, I'm your man. How would you go about hiring somebody here, anyway? You know less than nothing about safes, Lee. How would you know a guy was good enough if you couldn't even ask him if he wanted one lump or two? Use your bloody loaf; this is Italy. I'll open up this damn thing and then we'll get the hell back to the Smoke. We've a shop waiting."

I looked at him and nodded. "Thanks," I said. "Of course I need you, actually."

"I should bloody think you do."

"Did Selby point out that this involved murder?"

"He mentioned that Mister Big had to go, yes. It puts you out of a job, of course, but it makes no difference to me. If you agreed to it, that's good enough, Lee. You've got your reasons."

I looked at him again and shook my head. "Christ; that must be what they call faith," I said.

"I shouldn't wonder. So when are we doing the job?"

"As soon as possible, believe me. You know we're aiming to destroy a whole lot of files and suchlike?" Moleman nodded. "Well," I went on, "the problem is that we don't yet know if the stuff's even in Trieste."

"We've got to make sure of that," he agreed. "But Selby says it's significant how many other people in town think it's all up at Javits' warehouse."

"Selby said that?" I asked. "Where is he, for Pete's sake?"

"Right here."

"You might have told me. So might he, damn him. Well, okay. So who're all these other people supposed to be?"

Moleman shrugged. "Agents of sorts, I gather."

"Then, Jesus Christ," I said angrily, "why don't *they* go ahead and find out if Javits has the stuff here?"

"Well," said Moleman apologetically, "that's what I asked him, too. Selby said it's you they're all waiting for."

17

Jesus Christ, I thought angrily as I made my way back to the Hotel Sesana, Selby had bloody well gone and done it again. He'd got me into yet another mess while only telling me half the story. I was being used once again, this time to precipitate a crisis in order that he or his Agency could sit around and watch without getting their noses dirty. It was the age-old way of gathering information. Presumably he was wandering about the streets or holed up with a pair of binoculars somewhere just watching the agents pour into town and making notes. Cool old Selby.

I'd walked back with Moleman to his own hotel, which wasn't more than half a mile from my own.

"We start tomorrow?" he queried.

"Okay. How are you on opening doors nowadays? Big, solid metal doors with a combination lock in the middle and a safe-type handle, for instance."

Mole grinned. "I expect I could still make a living out of it," he said. "But those particular ones can be tricky," he added seriously. "It'll need planning. You'll have to find out some things about these doors tomorrow. For instance, what do the keys look like? Can you see a maker's name anywhere on the lock or the hinges or on the keys themselves? That could help a lot. Also, try to find out if when Javits and this Guido fellow lock up at night they leave the lights on inside the armory. Do they turn any master switches off anywhere?"

"Why do you want to know that?"

"Because the simplest way of insuring that nobody gets in is by cutting off the current. Those locks are worked by electricity. You could have both the bloody keys but you still wouldn't get in. I've seen those types before."

I had to admit that I mightn't have thought of that one.

"Also, see if you can find out if the combination lock on the other door has more than one ring to turn. Sometimes there's the knob in the middle, a calibrated inner portion and an outer ring that also goes round." He demonstrated with his hands.

"Okay, I'll see what I can do."

"Then tomorrow night we'll find out what it is that so many people are after."

"If it's there," I'd said gloomily.

But it was anger rather than gloom I felt as I walked home. I seemed to be spending my time being blackmailed or threatened into doing things I hadn't much inclination to do. It wasn't like that in the Army, I thought bitterly and quite irrelevantly. When I got in, I found a message waiting for me in the pigeonhole behind my key. I took it upstairs to read like some secretive teen-ager with a love letter. It was less than amorous.

Glad you're here and have met your ally. Deal must be completed by Friday evening latest. Will be keeping an eye out for you. S.

I had become all disorientated by moving around so much. I rang down to reception on the bedroom phone.

"What day is it today?" I asked.

"*Mercoledì.*"

"I was afraid of that."

So the following day, my first full day at work, I spent sneaking about when Guido's presence didn't make it necessary for me to be picking up one damned Iranian rifle after another and examining it cursorily. While he was standing there in his black tie and pointed shoes, a clipboard with a silver pencil held against his chest and a slight sneer on his face, I took down gun after gun. Unless they were in mint condition, I took out the bolts, looked at the bolt face and squinted down the barrel. That was while he was there. When he wasn't, I merely picked them out of the rack, glanced at them and put them back. I had no intention of wasting time and energy inspecting a load of weapons that were due to be blown sky-high before the next evening. Nevertheless, Guido had given me a trolley with canvas walls which I was supposed to fill with the weapons I rejected, so I had to be reasonably careful, especially as he was in the habit of popping up unexpectedly from behind a rack somewhere and looking at the weapons I had already inspected, running the end of his silver pencil from butt to butt with a clicking noise which made me want to push his teeth in even more than when we had first met.

But when I knew he was in one of the warehouses with Javits, or talking on the telephone in the Inquiries office at the front, I'd go and examine the locking system on the doors of the armory. They appeared to be made by a company called Kühn of Essen, and I made mental notes about the type of keys used. But it was not until the late afternoon that Javits decided to go into the vault he said was full of files and archives. From a distance I watched as he manipulated the dials on the combination lock, but they were screened by his body. When the heavy door was open, I saw that the steel frame in which it was hung had holes in it corresponding to bolts in the door itself. There were two at the top, three down the side and another two at the bottom. It was not the sort of door you could get through by kicking. While Javits was inside, a red light over the door came on in addition to the amber one that had started flashing as soon as the combination was moved. I wondered if the red light was connected to an infrared sensor inside that detected body heat.

I didn't feel I'd achieved much by the time I finished, but when I saw Moleman that evening he was pleased.

"Much as I thought," he said. "Javits isn't really scared he'll be burgled, you know. I'll bet you that none of those warning lights and sirens are connected to anywhere outside, such as his apartment up in Villa Opicina. That's extremely difficult to arrange with the authorities, as well as being impossibly expensive."

"I hope you're right," I said.

At about eleven o'clock, we walked down to the warehouses. It was comparatively early, but Moleman thought it might take some time to get in and that it was best to have as much as possible of the night before us. We were both dressed in dark clothes, and he was carrying a bulky leather case containing his tools and some demolition equipment which Selby had given him that afternoon. When we reached the wharf, the place was in darkness. From up the road came the sounds people make at night in Mediterranean countries; a radio was going, a man was shouting and some children were playing in the street. Presumably they slept by day. But down by the warehouses all was quiet, with just the lapping of water against the piles of the wharf. The big sign saying EDERA S.A. glimmered above the entrance. Immediately behind the warehouses rose the black bulk of the hill. Not a light showed anywhere.

We walked quietly around the side, but there were no other entrances, although we did find an iron ladder bolted to the wall and leading up to the pitched roofs. I remembered that there had been no skylights, so presumably it gave access for repair or maintenance work such as clearing the gutters. We returned to the front, and Moleman got busy on the door marked INFORMAZIONE. It took him thirty seconds before he pushed it open and we went in, closing it behind us. We stood in the darkness for a moment, listening.

"No lights yet," he said softly.

"Okay. The door into the warehouse is over on the right here."

This door was metal and also locked; it took Moleman a couple of minutes' work in the pencil beam of a flashlight which I held. There was no doubt that he was good at the simple stuff. I clicked off the light before opening the door and stepping into the darkened warehouse. This time we left the door slightly ajar. The air was still and cold and smelled of petrol and oil from the Ferret cars. There was still no sound, so Moleman turned on his torch again and I led him down the middle aisle to the back of the warehouse. Halfway down, he caught his foot in one of the railway lines and almost fell, his torch hand flailing round and hitting the armored front of one of the scout cars with a dull thump. He said something under his breath as we listened to the echoes dying away among the girders and gantries for traveling cranes overhead.

"Good solid doors, these," he commented approvingly when we reached the sliding gates that gave access to the underground armory. "I know this type, all right. I'd say they were installed about seven years ago. Since then Kühn's have brought out a different model which is much harder to open."

He flipped up the hatch of the wall panel, and the illuminated button glowed in the dark.

"Okay," he said. "The current's on. This'll take a bit longer." Moleman opened his leather case again and took out a wallet, which he unrolled on the cement floor. Having selected a screwdriver, he carefully unscrewed the panel immediately surrounding the locks and lifted it clear. "It's a bit elementary," he said. "Although the locks themselves are still in those capsules, all the wiring's now exposed." He reached into the box with a pair of cutters and snipped through a blue-and-white flex. "That's the siren out," he said.

After some fiddling, he found a couple of keys to fit both locks. While he worked, I held the torch and listened to the small sounds he made in the great silent volume of air all around. The occasional click and chink of metal, the crackle of a piece of grit underfoot—everything was magnified by the hollowness of the building. Then Moleman stood back.

"On the count of three, you turn that top key—all right?" I nodded and took hold of it. He counted, and we both turned simultaneously. Then, with his left hand, he pressed the glowing button. From somewhere in the wall came the muffled moan of an electric motor, and the doors slid

193

apart. There was no siren. Moleman gave a silent grin of self-satisfaction and picked up the panel cover from the floor. "Always replace what you remove," he said sententiously, screwing it back into the wall. "We'll mend that siren on the way out, though. No point in giving Javits clues. Right now, we go in." He picked up his roll of instruments and the bag, and we walked down the short, white-painted corridor into the vast man-made cavern under the hill. That familiar smell drifted out to meet us.

"Where are the light switches, Lee?" he asked.

"They're in four blocks. A and B one to six and seven to twelve; C and D one to six and seven to twelve. This place is a square divided into a grid. Halfway up the left side is the door we want. On the opposite side is the door to the magazine where Javits says he's got some demolition charges. I've seen it, but I haven't been in; the door's fireproof, but unlocked. The wind-down steel shutter type."

"All right." The pencil beam settled on a block of switches, and Moleman clicked down the one marked D6. Far away to the left, a single light came on behind the black bulks of gun racks.

"That'll do," I said. We walked round the outer aisle towards it.

"Hell of a big place," commented Moleman. "I suppose you're armed?" he asked suddenly.

"You're damn right I'm armed," I said. "Javits himself gave me the gun, and I helped myself to some of his own ammunition yesterday. You're not, though, are you?"

"No fear. Can't stand the things. At least, not on a job," he added.

It took him nearly three-quarters of an hour to open the door to Javits' strong room. He worked in total silence, listening to the tumblers with a stethoscope as well as monitoring the internal movements of the lock mechanism electronically. While he was busy, I took his torch and prowled about the armory. The only discovery I made was of an air vent about four feet up the rear wall. It had a circular louvered opening a couple of feet across. Curiosity made me undo the knurled screws that held on the venetian-blind arrangement. Inside there was a sudden drop of perhaps a yard, while above it a metal-lined shaft climbed vertically away. I presumed the drop below it was the equivalent to a plumber's U-bend, to act as a trap for water or stones or anything else that might fall in from above. I shone my torch down and saw some pebbles at the bottom, together with what had probably once been a bird's nest. Looking up the shaft, I could see the blades of a fan about six feet away. They were motionless, and on the wall beside the vent I found a switch which operated the motor to duct a gust of cool night air across my midriff. I wondered why there was only one ventilator, but decided that the volume of air in the place was so great that more than one was not necessary. I replaced the cover and went back to Moleman, who was putting his stethoscope away.

"Watch this," he said, and he pulled the door handle up. He threw his weight back, and slowly the door began to move outwards. The amber light winked on above it.

"You haven't lost the knack, then," I said.

"No," he said proudly. "I wouldn't claim to be able to open anything, but standard vault doors like this or those other locks, they're child's play. It just takes a bit of time and patience. Let's go and see what aces Mr. Javits has in his hand."

We went into the strong room then and turned on the

195

overhead light. It wasn't a very big place—perhaps eighteen feet square, and most of that space taken up by a bank of gray filing cabinets along one wall. There were also a steel desk and a padded swivel chair. On the whitewashed concrete wall above the desk hung a large photograph of a woman's face. She was of indeterminate age—somewhere between fifty and eighty: the skin very lined and wrinkled, making it seem more likely to be eighty, except that the eyes were so bright and hard. The left eyelid drooped slightly, as did the left corner of her mouth. It had to be Mama; even without the black crape around the picture, it'd have had to be Mama.

"Twenty past midnight," I said. "You made good time, Mole."

"Not bad," he said modestly. "Would've been better a few years ago, but it's still not bad. Who's the old bird?" He jerked a thumb at the photo.

"Javits' mother. Let's get on with it."

Moleman made short work of the locks at the top of each column of drawers. I opened one and saw almost at a glance that we'd found what we were looking for. I took the gun out of my pocket and handed it to him.

"There's no need for you to see this stuff, Mole," I said. "Much better not, in fact. Here, take this and patrol a bit in the armory. Someone might come along. Give me a few minutes."

"Okay, Lee." He took the gun and vanished.

It became clear right from the start that Javits' *Vulcan Bulletins* would be gripping reading. The files were not indexed by country, but only by the names of the people concerned. There were ministers, generals, agents, even presidents. Most of the names were unknown to me, and many had *Deceased* written in red ink next to them. Some however, were household names, although the dates of their first entries were of days when they had been unknown and distinguished only by ambitiousness and opportunism. Many of the records were, in fact, beautifully chronicled accounts of men who had risen from obscurity by means of an ever-increasing devotion to expediency; their methods ranged from petty venality right through to blackmail and murder. Here was a Swiss Government official who had helped executives in the Oerlikon arms company to obtain forged end-use papers in order to export Swiss antiaircraft guns to Federal Nigeria during the Nigerian Civil War. Here was the American four-star general whose networks of operations in Southeast Asia had enabled him to keep the Viet Cong supplied with American 81mm mortar bombs during the 1968 Tet Offensive; here was the Senator who'd known. Here was one of the directors of a British company of gun dealers who had worked out the involved shuffle through six different countries of ten thousand automatic pistols destined for Rhodesia at a time when sanctions legislation made it illegal. Here were a thousand ordinary men, as well as a handful of fairly extraordinary women, who knew a great deal about the way the world was actually run. Here, among them, was Anscudden.

I pulled out his file and flipped through it. Javits had done his homework well: the first entry was dated way back in the late Fifties, the day Timothy Anscudden had unwittingly completed his first arms transaction. It went on to record the names of the businessmen with whom he had associated in Hong Kong and who had an active interest in the drug trade. That Javits kept his files meticulously up to date was proved by the last entry, which recorded the whole

Trebizond fiasco. There was a note afterwards in green ink: *Deceased Malta. Mutilated by Libyans in reprisal.* Enclosed in the folder was a plain manila envelope containing half a dozen glossy color photographs, presumably taken in a hotel bedroom considerably east of Suez. Most of the boys in the pictures looked less than fifteen; one or two were probably no more than nine or ten. They were quite good pictures; presumably one of Anscudden's little friends had made free with his Polaroid camera while the owner's attention was distracted. The definition of the ex-Major's naked body was excellent, as was that of everyone else in the pictures. I thought the kids were probably Malaysians, and then slipped the photos back into Anscudden's folder.

My own file was much less spectacular; a prosaic account of many of my arms deals dating from after I'd left the Army. I assumed the record was sketchy because several of the deals had been too insignificant to bother with. In such company I was completely outclassed. There were one or two cross-references to contacts I knew in armaments centers such as Frankfurt and Brussels, including my Viennese friend who made sporting rifles out of surplus hardware. It was all pretty undistinguished.

Moleman looked in.

"What's the time?" he asked.

"Coming up to one."

"I'm going across to look at the explosives in the magazine room. We want some charges that will rip these cabinets open so the incendiary can get to work."

"What are you using?" I asked. He opened his fat leather bag.

"RDX," he said. "I brought a few detonators along, and four timers. I'll see what else I can find over the way." He closed the bag and put it on the desk before picking up his torch and going quietly out. I noticed that he had half-obscured a magazine with the bag, and a corner of it caught my attention. I went over and pulled it out, and it was a mock-up of the first number of Javits' journal. The cover had been professionally done to look reminiscent of the *Time* format, with the *Vulcan Bulletin* masthead in red and below it in white the subtitle "Monthly Journal of the International Society for Political Truth." Most of the cover below that was a blank square in which, presumably, a photograph or art design would fit.

Left alone, I had one more piece of information to look up. I went to the filing cabinets and found Selby's file. It took me a minute or two fully to appreciate the significance of much that it contained, and a further ten minutes to commit it to memory. Then I put it back, and as I was straightening up, a voice from the doorway said, "Hold it, mister" in best Hollywood style, so I held it.

Guido was standing just inside the strong room pointing an automatic at me. I thought at first it was the 1911 Colt .45, but then light caught the print on the left side of the gun, GABILONDO Y CIA, and I recognized it as a Llama, a cheaper Spanish copy.

"I always have doubts of you, mister," said Guido. "Now I know." He was wearing training shoes, I noticed; otherwise he hadn't changed.

"I think we ring Mr. Javits, no?" he said, moving further into the room.

"No," said Mole's voice behind him.

Instead of doing the sensible thing—which would have been to freeze, drop the Llama and shrug expressively—Guido decided to be a hero. He spun and blasted off a shot which barely made it through the doorway. Moleman, from half behind the wall on his left, had a clean measured shot, which took Guido in the chest and slammed him back against the filing cabinets, his head striking the front with a metallic boom. Guido sat down slowly, with his mouth open and his eyes fixed on Moleman. He gave a little cough and died. Some blood ran down his chin onto his black tie.

"Thanks," I said.

"Did I do that?" asked Moleman nervously. His hand was shaking; by no means a born killer.

"That was a fellow called Guido. Javits' storeman." Moleman dipped his head and quickly gave me back the pistol.

"He may have known about guns, but he didn't know much about shooting. What are we going to do with him?"

"We'll have to dump him somewhere when we've finished. Let's just put him outside for the moment." When we lifted Guido, he farted, as the newly dead often do. We propped him up against the wall outside the strong room.

"Right," said Moleman when that was done. "We can start setting the charges if you've finished doing your blackmail homework. How much space have we got in the bottom of those cabinets?"

We removed a bottom drawer. Underneath there was a gap of about nine inches.

"You could get some plastic into there," I said. He nodded and molded a sausage out of RDX, which he laid on the floor at the back. He took a detonator out of his bag and pushed the terminals into the plastic explosive and then finally connected the detonator to a small timer which, I saw, was made in West Germany and calibrated up to twenty-four hours.

"When do you want it timed for?" he asked.

"Seventeen hundred hours tomorrow," I said. "I heard Javits tell Guido he wouldn't be coming in before lunch. Apparently he never leaves before about seven anyway."

"You want it to be dark, then?"

"Yes," I said. "People are going to ask questions about this: you can't blow up a bloody great arms depot without the police nosing round. They'll dispose of the accident theory just as soon as they get their experts in. I know who I want under suspicion while I'm getting the hell out of Trieste."

"Who?"

"Croatian saboteurs—same as the guys who blew up the oil dump a couple of months back and not a million miles from here."

"Who're they?" asked Moleman. "Politicos?"

"I don't know." I shrugged. "The press describes them as nationalists—which, if I know anything, means right-wing opportunists. But they'll make ideal fall guys. And they tend to work at night. We want to make it as authentic as possible."

"Okay," said Moleman. He carefully set the timer for 1700 hours, pressed the switch that activated it and placed it at the back of the filing cabinet. "You can't turn these off, you know," he added. "If you want to stop it exploding, you have to dismantle the whole thing."

"I shan't want to," I said. Together we replaced the heavy drawer, put the stops back on the slides that prevented it from being withdrawn by accident and shut it. Then we relocked the whole cabinet. We checked that we had left nothing in the room before going out.

"Good night, Mama," I said to the picture above the desk as I switched off the light.

Moleman closed the heavy door and spun the combination lock.

"What are we going to do with him?" I asked, jerking a thumb at Guido.

"There are some tall racks in the explosives room. We could put him behind those. I doubt if anybody ever looks behind them."

"No, but if they were going to, they'd certainly pick tomorrow to do it. I've got a better place."

We picked up the dead man and carried him to the far end of the armory.

"We'll stuff him in the ventilator," I said. "I found it while you were opening the door." As we put him down on the floor again, Moleman tucked Guido's Llama into the man's jacket pocket. I undid the screws and removed the cover again. Mole peered inside with his flashlight.

"Ideal."

We bundled Guido into the trap inside, along with the bird's nest and the pebbles, and I replaced the front.

It was nearly two when we began setting the other charges. Moleman had cranked up the fireproof door of the magazine, and inside was a large cold box of a room with rough gray cement walls and the inevitable NO SMOKING signs. There were also some felt overshoes and instructions to remove all metal objects from the pockets just inside the door. We ignored this and set about removing demolition charges from their boxes. In one crate we found canvas satchels containing Claymore mines, and we emptied that as well. Then we loaded as much as we could onto a rubber-tired trolley and moved off to lay it.

"Where do we put it?" I asked.

"There'll be a hell of a blast when the magazine goes up,

but there's a lot of space in this hall which'll slightly diminish the effect. We need a charge that'll blow the main doors out to let air in for the incendiaries to take a hold. What's the nearest stack to the main entrance?"

"Either B-one or C-one," I said. "The one on the left is a couple of tons of UN steel helmets. The other's something in boxes, but I can't remember what."

It turned out, by a stroke of luck, to be 81mm mortar bombs. We removed some of the boxes from the pile until we came to the hollow in the middle of the racks. Mole climbed in, and I passed him the demolition charges and Claymore mines one by one.

"I'm stacking the mines so that the blast is all concentrated in one direction," he called, his voice muffled.

"Fine." When Claymores explode, they throw out a scythe of metal in a fixed arc, and they can be fired electrically if necessary. I remembered seeing them effectively deployed in the Mekong Delta round the forts scattered in the outback. These forts were sometimes manned by Green Berets, but more often by South Vietnamese Regional Forces and Popular Forces—RFs and PFs, nicknamed Rough Puffs. The Rough Puffs usually constructed their forts of mud and concrete in the shape of large triangles, surrounding them with accordion wire, barbed wire and a few lines of Claymore mines. If the Viet Cong were spotted approaching, the men in the fort would wait until they were fairly close to the walls and then trigger the whole bank of Claymores at once. This was extremely effective at first, but it wasn't long before the Viet Cong had cottoned on to digging up the Claymores, turning them round and putting them back again. It was a nasty shock for the Rough Puffs. The only sort of answer to that is to use nondirectional mines like

Bouncing Bettys, which are not the sort of weapons you play tricks with. They leap out of the ground to about face height before exploding. They're a whole lot worse than an attack of acne.

"I've rigged them to fire simultaneously," called out Moleman. "It'd be a bad mistake to choose that moment to come through the door." He climbed out again, bent double, and we replaced the boxes of mortar bombs. "Nobody'll see that." He nodded in satisfaction. "Now just a charge in the magazine and some incendiaries, and the job's done." He went back and fused some RDX strategically hidden on the underside of several shelves. "Now"—he looked around the armory—"what else have we got that'll burn?"

We walked briskly around, stopping only to plant one of three small white phosphorus bombs under the pile of inflatable rubber dinghies. Two more went among ammunition boxes and the stack of fifty-gallon drums of paint that Javits was presumably keeping for the Ferrets. Then, at the last moment, we came on a block of shelves full of oddments, "one-offs" and other separate items that Javits had picked up here and there. Several of them I recognized as weaponry being used by the Americans in Southeast Asia—particularly small underwing missiles used in strike aircraft or gunships like the Hueys. There were ten 2.75 HVARs—high-velocity aircraft rockets—which had fins that folded. There was also a lengthy canister that would fit inside one of the Genie Magnum air-to-surface missiles or that could be dropped separately. It was a CBU, or cluster bomb unit. The CBU was filled with metal balls, and inside each metal ball was a number of bomblets, which were smaller metal balls. The CBUs were scattered by compressed air across a target; with a bit of practice, a skilled pilot could achieve a very close pattern, which at night sparkled prettily and which could shred any living thing within range. The nastiest bomblets were the delayed-action ones, which could explode hours or even days later.

"It's a pleasure to be sending this lot up through the roof," I said. We pushed the last phosphorus bomb in among these sophisticated items.

"The heat'll do the rest," said Moleman.

We went back to the magazine, checked it, turned out the lights and cranked down the door. It was just after half past three. Mole picked up his bag, and we walked back to the main entrance. It was curious knowing that scattered strategically among the tons of ordnance and equipment in this underground cavern were timing devices humming quietly away as their tiny battery-powered electric clock mechanisms wound off the seconds towards the moment when one contact was broken and another closed.

I had a last look round before turning off the single light shining away outside Javits' strong room. All I noticed was a faint smell of cordite in the air. I put it down to imagination, for Mole's single shot could hardly have accounted for it. We went back through the still-open doors, and he unscrewed the panel behind the flap again. I pushed the button that closed the doors, and he set about repairing the siren. When he had joined the wires again, he replaced the panel and closed the cover.

"What'll you do tomorrow?" he asked as we walked back through the lines of scout cars.

"Make sure Javits is here in the afternoon and keep him here until five," I said. "If I have to, I suppose I'll shoot the bugger myself and leave him."

"I'll be watching," said Moleman.

"Thanks, Mole. You'll keep people out of the way? You know, kids and passersby. And discourage visitors from coming through that *Informazione* door—because otherwise they might get a lot more than a Javits Corporation brochure."

"I'll need a hand, I think," he said. "I can't be everywhere at once, and I sure as hell don't want to be standing right outside the front at five o'clock tomorrow, and that's a fact."

"Okay, get someone. Selby might help. Play it by ear."

"I reckon I'll also arrange to have someone standing on the hill to one side. They can toss a rock down onto the warehouse roof if you're not out by quarter to. A stopped watch could knacker you properly, and no mistake. D'you reckon you'll hear it inside?"

"I hope not," I said feelingly. "I hope by then I'll be some distance away. But if I'm still inside and it's a good-sized rock, I'll hear it."

Moleman locked the doors behind us, and we emerged into the cold night air outside the office. Except for the gentle noise of seawater, there was complete silence around us, which was only intensified by the far-off barking of a dog.

"You can tell it's not England, can't you?" he said on the way home. "It doesn't sound right." Then his stocky figure disappeared into the darkness, leather bag in one hand.

I made my way back to my own hotel along deserted streets full only of cats and garbage, a smell of sardines drifting up from the port.

18

In the morning, the first thing I did was write a careful letter on hotel notepaper, which had a lot of blue print at the top, together with an idealized sketch of the Hotel Sesana. I then went along to the main post office and registered it before sending it on its way.

I thought there wasn't much point in going to the warehouses if Javits himself was not going to be there until after lunch. There wouldn't be anyone else around except Guido, and I knew where he was. I thought of him in there screwed up at the bottom of the ventilation shaft while electric timers hummed away unheard in the darkness nearby. Despite my inclination not to go near the place ever again, I finally went down in response to the old Army training which makes it obligatory to have an exact knowledge of how the land lies. I walked up the hill and stood on the top, looking out over Muggia Bay and the city. Behind me, the ranges of hills rose towards Yugoslavia. A couple of hundred feet exactly below me lay the vast armory excavated from the heart of the hill; I could look down towards the waterfront and see the tarred black roofs of the twin warehouses jutting out side by side from the base of the hill. Near me was a clump of bushes, and in the middle I could make out the shape of a large cement mushroom. It was probably the nearest thing to a tombstone Guido was likely to get.

When it was midday, I took the H&K VP-70 out of my pocket and checked the load. Eighteen in the magazine and one in the chamber. I hoped I wouldn't need any of them. I slipped it back and went down the hill to kill time with a plate of spaghetti and a glance to see what Michelangelo was up to today. I couldn't remember if I had last left him being agonized or ecstatic.

I was back waiting outside *Informazione* when Javits turned up, with Frick driving.

"Hi there," he said. "Why don't you go on in?"

"It's locked," I said.

"The hell it is. Where's Guido?"

"I don't know." I shrugged. "He isn't around today."

"The hell he ain't." Javits strode to the door and rattled it before mashing a white thumb down on the bell, which could be heard ringing inside. "Aw, shit," said Javits finally. "We'll have to go and root out that mother. Lee, you mind sticking around here in case he turns up? Frick and me'll go visit his apartment. Maybe we'll have to go pick up my other key from Villa Opicina. Shit."

He drove back again half an hour later. He was alone, I was glad to see. I'd forgotten all about Frick when planning today.

"Frick's hunting up Guido," said Javits. "Can't think where that mother's got to. Goddam wops. He's probably chasing a piece of tail." He seemed angry and put out. "Never mind," he said as he unlocked the office door; "forget him. I've got my other key." We walked through the echoing warehouse. "Must paint those scout cars," said Javits as we reached the armory doors. "If I don't get it done soon, they'll be too obsolete even for Tanzania. Got bigger things on my mind just now, though."

"The *Vulcan Bulletins?*" I said.

"Right on the button. Now, this here's a duplicate of Guido's key. Take it and do it just like you saw us do yesterday, huh?"

On the count of three we inserted our keys, then turned them, and Javits opened the sliding doors. The siren began its mournful wail, thank God, and I followed Javits in, leaving my key in the lock. Javits, I noticed, brought his with him and left it in the inside lock as he had previously. It was evidently one of those little rituals that develop from long usage. He didn't bother to push the button that closed them, but before striding rapidly off towards his strong room, he reached down and touched a concealed switch I hadn't noticed earlier that turned the siren off.

"I suggest you get busy, Lee," he called over one shoulder. "We've both got a hell of a way to go."

I fetched a trolley and started dumping Iranian rifles into it. This time I hardly bothered to distinguish between good and bad condition; all I wanted was to keep a background noise of activity going so that Javits would think I was occupied. I wanted very much to walk straight out and press the button that closed the doors behind me. Javits with his single key would then damn well have to stay there until five o'clock; but there was always the risk of the unexpected occurring, such as the surprise appearance of another Corporation employee like Guido. I wanted out of the whole business; I wanted it more than anything else, and the only way I could guarantee it was to make sure personally that Javits was down here when the magazine blew. As I worked, I found myself glancing more frequently at my watch and also looking back towards the entrance. I was on block C7, practically at the center of the armory. To my left at the end of a concrete alley was the door of Javits' strong room. Behind me, at the end of a broad avenue, were the sliding double doors, and near them the huge stack of 81mm mortar bombs which concealed the heap of fused Claymores and demolition charges. It was as if I expected to see a thin column of smoke rising from the middle of the stack; but of course there was nothing—no sign of the compact electric timer winding off the last half-hour.

I became suddenly aware that I wasn't alone as I worked. I looked up and Javits was watching me, leaning up against some nearby shelves. In his hands he held a buff folder which I recognized as being identical to the files in his cabinet. I nodded to him and went on working uneasily.

"Know who I saw in town today?" he asked suddenly.

"No idea," I said, snicking off a safety catch.

"Your friend Selby."

I looked up. "Good Lord," I said, "I never knew he was here."

"Didn't you, now? Well, ever since then I've been wondering what in hell could have brought him to Trieste."

"Perhaps he came to collect his money from you," I suggested. "You still owe him for staying aboard the *Marmara* as far as Gibraltar, remember."

Javits didn't answer. He stood there, one corner of the file tapping against his white teeth, while I grimly went on taking the bolts out of a lot of old Persian rifles and trying not to look at my watch. Javits' thick lips closed abruptly as he suddenly stepped forward, picking one of the guns out of the trolley.

"That's a mint-condition weapon, Lee," he said. "What in hell's got into you? It's not pitted or corroded or anything. You weren't like this yesterday; you sick or something?"

"It's a hybrid, Mr. Javits," I said patiently. "The number on the bolt doesn't correspond with the number on the receiver."

"Then that makes you a neurotic, Lee—a fucking perfectionist. Either that or you've got something on your mind. Like Mr. Selby."

"Look, Javits," I said. "I don't go a bundle on this temperamental stuff. If you don't like my work then that's one thing, but there's a limit to how far you can go poking around into people's lives for your own ends. Sooner or later, somebody's going to get fed up. I thought that on Malta, standing in that warehouse in front of poor bloody Anscudden, cross-examining him for you. And for what? A man in your line of business should know better than to ask too many personal questions."

"Yeah," said Javits, "maybe he should, at that. And I'll bet there's not a single person who gets a mention in my journal who hasn't said that maybe a thousand times in his life. I believe in truth, Lee, and so did my mom. She was *unable* to lie, you know that?"

"Like George Washington. Except that he once lied about his age."

"My mom was above petty vanity, Mr. McGundrell. Not only could she not tell a lie, but she had the effect on other people of making them truthful as well. D'you mind coming with me for a moment? Oh, forget those damned guns, huh?" he added, and I replaced a rifle in the rack.

He led me down the alley towards the door of his strong room, where he paused suddenly and peered at the nearest

211

rack of weapons, which happened to be old Canadian Ross .303s. It was practically a quarter to five, and I was shortly going to have to hit the man over the head.

"What do you reckon did that?" he asked, pointing at something with a thick white forefinger. There was a long pale groove running across the stock of one of the rifles, pointing towards the middle of the racks. I bent down a bit and saw what I expected to see: a hole rather less than half an inch wide which corresponded to the groove.

"Looks like a bullet," I said. It was obviously the shot from Guido's Llama that he had loosed off at Moleman.

"You're damn right it looks like a bullet. What I want to know is, who's been firing shots down here in my armory?"

"Perhaps your storekeeper could answer that," I said.

"When I find Guido, it's just one more damn question I'll be asking him," said Javits. Suddenly, his tone changed. He paused with his hand on the strong-room door. "I don't allow people in here, as a rule," he said. "It's kinda sacred in a way, because I guess it's here that I feel Mom's influence strongest. If you feel a smartass comment coming on, Mr. McGundrell, I'd suppress it firmly if I were you."

With a last menacing glare of his pinkish eyes, Javits hauled back, and the heavy door swung open. The room inside looked exactly as it had when Mole and I had left it some twelve hours before. There was no evidence that Javits had been doing any work at all. The filing drawers were all locked shut, and even the desk was bare, the mock-up of the cover of issue No. 1 of his *Vulcan Bulletins* having been tidied away somewhere. Only the folder he carried showed that he had any work on hand. I began to get a crawling sensation at the base of my spine and round my anus. I was running out of time very fast now. I glanced covertly at my watch again, and it was nearly ten minutes to five. The crawling sensation spread until I itched all over. Only one of the timing mechanisms had to be slightly inaccurate for me to be part of a very nasty explosion.

"You'll just excuse me first," I said to Javits. "I have to go to the john. I'll be right back."

Javits looked at me. His broad, flattish nose gleamed, I noticed irrelevantly; probably overactive sebaceous glands.

"You ain't going anywhere," he said. "Not until you've told Mama what your friend Selby's doing in town and why you're acting so goddam suspicious." He indicated the black-draped photograph hanging above the desk with a reverent gesture. "You'll stand in front of Mama and explain to both of us just what in hell's going on; and I'll be watching your eyes, McGundrell, because Mama makes people betray themselves through their eyes. Now, look at her; raise your right hand and sw—" He broke off, and I turned to look at him. Javits' attention was fixed on the floor in front of the filing cabinets. I followed the direction of his gaze and saw it: a small spot of dried blood which had obviously dripped unnoticed off Guido's tie.

"There's something damned odd been going on here," said Javits, straightening up. "That's blood, and I sure as hell haven't been bleeding in here." He looked up at the scrawny old bird on the wall. "Mama tells me you know something about all this, mister," he said quietly.

I began backing out of the strong room. The time had come to get out regardless; I wasn't going to get myself blown up for this albino maniac. Outside, I turned and ran up the alleyway to where I had been working. Just as I reached the trolley of Iranian rifles, I heard a familiar sound behind me and a voice shout, "Hold it!" I snatched a glance over one shoulder and knew I didn't have a hope in hell. Javits had grabbed a weapon from somewhere and was up on aim. I skidded abruptly to a halt. It was a rifle I knew, an Armalite AR-18. Small bullets, only .223 inch in caliber, but twenty of them in the magazine and each one with a velocity of over 3200 feet per second. You can't hope to outrun them.

I stood there with my hands raised while Javits came up with the Armalite at the ready.

"I only wanted the john," I said.

"That bad?" He patted my waistband and removed the VP-70. "I'll take this back," he said. "Giving things away for free can be corrupting." He put it in his pocket, and at that moment there came from beyond the main entrance a heavy metallic booming followed by a faint scrabbling sound. "Holy heck," said Javits, "they're on the roof."

I was too slow. I was still turning when he swung the rifle flat, and it caught me low in the stomach. As I doubled up, I could see the heels of his shoes dwindling fast up the broad concrete avenue. I blearily noticed my watch: eight minutes to five. Bloody Moleman and his fifteen minutes' warning! I was back on my feet and trying to run as Javits reached the entrance. He looked back, and for a moment I thought he was going to shoot me, but instead he yelled, "Frick can handle you!" His great white hand swept out and smashed down on the wall button. The heavy double doors began sliding silently together behind him.

Panic overcame the burning pain in my stomach as I tore down the avenue. Twenty yards to go, and I could still see the lines of Ferrets in the warehouse beyond, their matte desert finish pale beneath the powerful roof lights. Five yards and the view had shrunk to a strip of ocher two feet across and narrowing. Then my outstretched palms smacked into the doors, jarring my wrists, and there was no view at all except of a cold expanse of green-painted steel.

Outside it would be almost dark, the harbor lights twinkling on the black water and the Vittoria lighthouse flashing a few kilometers up the coast. Moleman would be pacing up and down, hopefully keeping the narrow road clear of passersby, looking at his watch with increasing frequency and wondering where the hell I'd got to.

Desperately I tried to turn Javits' key in the lock of the door-release panel, but it wouldn't turn on its own; the doors remained fast. Quick and unwilling look at the time: seven minutes in which to defuse all the charges. It couldn't be done, and part of my brain knew this and accepted it, but the other part was far more insistent that of course it was possible. Four timers to stop, one minute and forty-five seconds for each. The nearest was a few yards away, but it was buried in a stack of heavy cases of mortar bombs. I tore wildly at the boxes, splitting my fingernails and bringing several boxes toppling onto the floor, where one of them burst open, scattering bombs everywhere. My whole body winced and itched with apprehension as I worked desperately to open up a hole in the stack. I didn't dare look at my watch. I knew now that I wasn't going to make it, but I didn't want to discover by how much. I was about to be blown apart, which was quite bad enough without knowing the ironic margin by which I might have survived had I been more ruthless with Javits sooner, had he not hit me with the AR-18, had I not left the spare key in the other lock on the wrong side of those steel doors . . .

It was at that instant that I remembered Guido's key. He wore it on a chain; I had seen him take it out and use it. I was running well before I had even finished the train of thought, tearing down the broad concrete avenue, which seemed to stretch out for miles ahead before it ended in the distant blank wall. As I ran, I snatched a quick glimpse at my watch. Jesus Christ, the minute hand had passed the eleven already; less than five minutes. I flung myself towards the louvered cover of the ventilator, reaching for the knurled screws that held it shut. It seemed to take an age to unscrew them; the threads appeared to be a yard long, and all I could do was stand and fiddle with them while my imagination built up an intolerable feeling of pressure in the huge room at my back. Finally the screws came loose, and I ripped off the cover. It was dark inside the vent, but I reached in, and my hands got hold of Guido's hair. I wrenched his head up by the scalp, by the nose and anything else I could get a grip on. One of his cold earlobes started to tear, but then I got a firm grasp of his collar with the other hand and heaved his curled body up out of the little pit. I pulled him through the vent, and he fell the four feet to the floor, his head landing with a noise like that of a wooden bowling ball being dropped. I tore at his jacket, and there, inside, was that blessed silver chain, which broke as I ripped it out. On the end was the precious key.

The run back to the main entrance was endless, and I shouted curses at myself for having left the bloody trolley of rifles slap in the middle of the avenue. I dodged round it, and finally I was back again, skipping over the mortar bombs scattered round the steel doors. I put Guido's key in the second keyhole, turned both keys and pressed the glowing button with my chin. It wasn't a miracle, but it seemed like one as slowly the doors began to open. I was through them before they were more than eighteen inches apart, and I sure as hell wasn't about to stop and push the CLOSE button.

I ran up between the parked Ferrets, taking care not to catch my feet in the sunken railway lines. Thank God Javits hadn't hung around to shut the door through to the office, either, and I burst through, knocking over a goddam electric fan that some silly bugger had left behind it. Then I was out and running through the sweet night air, which had never smelled so beautifully of sardines before and probably never would again. I was in the center of a great lull when time and movement were frozen. The road was empty, the ripples in the harbor weren't moving and there was complete silence; I couldn't even hear my own panting gasps or the slap of my feet on the concrete apron in front of the warehouses.

I ran diagonally, obeying the directions of my subconscious, which knew that the blast would travel straight outwards. I was barely eighty yards away when I snatched a glance back over my left shoulder to check my position. Quite a lot of light was reflected from the center of Trieste, and it was anyway not yet completely dark. On top of the warehouses, tiny above the white capitals spelling out EDERA s.a., stood the figure of Javits still holding the AR-18. He must have been seventy feet aboveground, and he'd done well to climb the narrow iron ladder one-handedly. It was hardly the moment for belated warnings, but something made me shout.

"Javits!" I yelled.

The figure turned abruptly and paused as if he had difficulty in identifying the man he knew to be locked in the armory beneath the hill. Then he began to raise the rifle.

Different kinds of explosives differ widely in their effect, according to requirements. A demolition charge is formulated to have a "brisant" effect, which is its power to shatter, by containing explosives that have a very high detonation velocity and that consequently produce a powerful shock wave. This type of reaction is usually too violent to be useful as a propellant. The nitrocellulose-based compounds mostly used in cartridges burn more evenly and coolly, producing a large but consistent volume of gas. Altogether and in various forms, Javits' armory contained several different types of explosive, producing, each at its own speed and pound for pound, different amounts of heat, gas and pressure.

But even the experts called in afterwards by the Italian police were unable to determine which charge had exploded first. Whichever it was, I saw a brief stab of light leap up from the top of the dark hill's bulk like an exclamation mark. In the split second it took for the huge crimson flash to burst from under the edges of the roof and through chinks and crevices in the doors of the warehouses, all four charges must have released their energy and the chain reaction must have been well on its way. There was a moment just before Javits should have started firing when a sheet of light burst up at his feet, and then I distinctly saw both warehouses bulge before disintegrating. There was a moment of blank confusion in which violent impressions of light and sound ended in my struggling feebly in the cold water of the harbor while debris rained hissing down into the sea all around.

Somehow I swam the twenty yards to the wharf. Luckily, there was a ladder stapled to the balks of timber, and I dragged myself dizzily up it, retching seawater and with the feeling of having had felt stuffed into both ears. By the time I was on the quay again, the heat of the fire was almost too intense for me even at a hundred yards. The warehouses had disappeared, and where they had stood was a cleared space. The neat lines of scout cars had vanished. Most of the Ferrets had been blown forward by the blast and were now piled together along the road and right on the quay itself in a tangle of armor plating and still-spinning wheels.

At the base of the hill was a torn hole which had once been the neat rectangular opening holding the sliding doors. Inside was a searing white inferno. One side of the hill had been blasted out, and flames were roaring out with a sound like a giant blowlamp. A bright jet of flame was also jutting from the mouth of the ventilator shaft two hundred feet up on top. I dragged my eyes away from this spectacle and suddenly caught sight of Moleman, running along the quay towards me, dodging the wrecked scout cars, with one arm thrown up to protect his face from the heat.

"Are you okay?" he shouted as he came up. His face was covered in earth, and his coat was ripped in several places. I could barely hear him.

"Probably," I yelled back.

He caught hold of my arm and pulled me away out of the direct heat and glare. I noticed that the ground was littered with unexploded rounds of ammunition which had simply been hurled through the doorway by the blast.

"I saw you go into the sea," he panted.

"More than I did. I woke up in it."

"Christ, that was some bang." Moleman stopped and looked back at the blazing ruins of the little hill. "I saw Javits go up to the roof," he said.

"He'll have come down by now, I expect."

"Yes," said Moleman uncertainly. "You did say he was a villain?"

"Mad and bad," I assured him. "But he loved his mother." Moleman nodded.

"I reckon we'd better scarper," he said. The first dazed

spectators were beginning to arrive, and from the distance came the panting wail of an emergency vehicle.

"Bloody Croat saboteurs," I said. "They'll do anything to attract a bit of attention." I was feeling light-headed. Some of the felt stuffed into my ears was coming loose, and I could hear a bit better. "Incidentally, what the hell kept you so long with that bloody warning signal?"

Moleman looked sheepish. "He couldn't find anything to throw," he said. "There weren't any stones lying about up on the hill."

"Who?"

"I dunno. Some kid I found. I gave him my watch and a handful of their funny-money and told him to get on with it. When nothing happened, I ran up and there he was, silly bugger, looking for something to throw."

"What did you do?"

"Hell, I grabbed his dog and threw that. I'd have thrown him too if he hadn't been wearing my watch."

We turned up a side street. "Thanks a lot, Mole," I said simply. "That's it, then. You piss off back to London now as fast as you can; just go right now—don't wait for anything. I'll see you back in the shop whenever."

"Don't mind if I do," he said. "This spaghetti's getting me down. It feels like I've been eating knitting."

19

Walking back to the Hotel Sesana was strange, because everybody else was going in the opposite direction. It seemed that all Trieste was converging on the ruins of the Javits Corporation. On the way, I saw Frick abandoning his car in a jam and setting off at a run. His face wore the sick look of a bodyguard who knows he hasn't done enough guarding. I was just reaching for the gun Javits had taken when he spotted me and stopped. His own pistol appeared in his hand. He stood there uncertainly, pointing it at me while all around us excited citizens were hurrying down to the quay to see the fun.

"You?" he asked, jerking his head in that direction. I nodded.

"He's dead," I said. "He was standing on the roof when the place blew."

Frick looked at his pistol for a moment, then shrugged his shoulders and put it away.

"Then I guess, as he's no longer paying my bill, I no longer work for him," he said, and he walked off.

But not everybody in Trieste had gone. The desk clerk, in a delirium of rage at being unable to abandon his post and join in the excitement, scrabbled behind him and handed me my key without tearing his eyes from the open doorway past which people were hurrying.

"Thanks," I said. I stood there with seawater running out of my trousers into the foyer carpet, my hair plastered to my head and my collar gaping. "Wind's freshening," I said. "I shouldn't be surprised if we had some rain before tomorrow." I don't believe he heard me, so I went up to my room, and there was Selby sitting on my bed reading Irving Stone.

"Jesus," he said, looking me up and down. "And this man thinks Michelangelo had problems." He tossed the book onto the bed. "I gather Javits is no more."

"How do you know?" I asked, peeling off my clothes exhaustedly and leaving them in a pile on the floor.

"It's all over town. The place is full of rollicking agents slapping their thighs."

"Fine. I can now go home."

"Well," said Selby, "there are one or two . . ."

"No." I held up a hand. "I don't want to know. I've done the bloody job and that's it."

"So what are you thinking of doing now, Lee?" he asked. "Going back to join the Army?"

I looked at him blankly.

"After nearly four years of freedom and free enterprise? Why the hell would I want to do that?"

"Come on, Lee," he said, "you know you've been bloody miserable since the day you left. You're one of those people that need the life. You like having your mates around you. You're no loner."

"Thanks, Doctor," I said. "They've been such wonderful mates, too." Selby grimaced at the bedspread. "But if I ever do decide to join up again," I told him, "you'll be the man I'll come to. You can help oil the wheels."

Selby looked surprised.

"Good heavens," he said, "I don't have that sort of pull."

I gave him a beautiful smile as I stepped out of my sodden underwear and drew back the shower curtain.

"Oh, yes you have," I said. "You could wield quite a clout if you wanted to. I've seen your record. The one Javits had."

I turned on the shower and luxuriated in the hot water. I emerged feeling better and found Selby lying back on the bed reading Irving Stone again.

"So I suppose you've written a letter," he said.

"Posted this morning."

"To be opened not later than the end of the month, sort of thing."

"That sort of thing," I agreed. " 'To whom it may concern.' "

"Awkward."

"You're damn right. It was a very detailed file. I don't suppose I forgot more than half of what was in it."

"Fuck you, Lee," he said dispassionately.

"Now you know how it feels. Let me warn you now, you never get used to it." I went over to the window. Over towards the sea there was a bright orange glow in the sky above the neighboring roof tops.

"Maybe," said Selby. That was all he said.

Not long afterwards, I looked up Captain Ratnayaka's shipping line in the Lloyd's list and sent him an envelope enclosing five hundred dollars in C bills. God knows why. I also wrote a note telling him I was thinking of going back into uniform. God knows why I did that either. Eventually I received an envelope that had been posted in Colón. In it were five hundred-dollar bills. There was no note of any kind. Who knows—a man of principle . . .